Man and His World

Man and His World

CLARK BLAISE

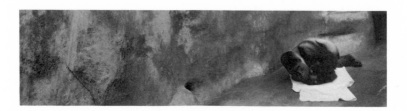

The Porcupine's Quill, Inc.

CANADIAN CATALOGUING IN PUBLICATION DATA

Blaise, Clark, 1940-
  Man and his world

ISBN 0-88984-148-9

I. Title.

PS8553.L34 1992   C813'.54   C92-094699-2
PR9199.3.B42M34 1992

Published by The Porcupine's Quill, Inc., 68 Main Street, Erin, Ontario N0B 1T0 with financial assistance from The Canada Council and the Ontario Arts Council.

Stories in this book have appeared in the following publications: *Lettre internationale* (French and Czech), *Salmagundi, Bomb, Toronto Life, Fiction International, New Virginia Review,* and *Descant*.

Distributed by General Publishing, 30 Lesmill Road, Co. Ltd., Don Mills, Ontario M3B 2T6.

Readied for the press by John Metcalf.
Copy edited by Doris Cowan.

Cover and title page photographs by Volker Seding.
The author photo is by Lem Torrevillas.

Typeset in Ehrhardt, printed and bound by The Porcupine's Quill. The stock is acid-free Zephyr Antique laid.

Second Printing 1993.

To the memory of parents, Lee R. Blaise (1905-1978)
and Anne V. Blaise (1903-1987)
And to my father-in-law, Sudhir Lal Mukherjee (1912-1985)

Contents

A Tour around My Father

MY FATHER'S NAME was Romeo, not uncommon in the time and place of his christening in Lac Mégantic, Québec, in 1905, but embarrassing enough for him to hide it. He went by his middle name, Leo, later 'Kid Leo' the Fighting French Featherweight. When he was a salesman and trying to latch on in the States, he became Lee, with Romeo buried behind an innocuous initial. He put a final vowel at the end of his name, to make it more pronounceable to Americans. I never knew him well, though his world is the psycho-magma of my worst dreams. My mother was his second, or perhaps even third wife, and there were two others after her.

He was the eighteenth child, the last son, and was given to the Church at birth, a *donné*, in the medieval tradition. He walked away from the Brothers in 1914 and never returned to schooling or to the Church. In the same year, one of his older brothers, christened Olivier but known as Bilou in the family, joined the Canadian Army and was shipped to France. He married there and never came back.

My father was a young man of many talents. As a brawler he was in demand by Montréal bootleggers during Prohibition. He sang in the bistros where Americans came to get their booze first-hand. He learned his English by imitating crooners, and in later life he sounded like Bing Crosby, and carried himself like a handsome George Raft. Alone, he was a sullen, torpid man who could sleep a weekend away. But before everything he was Romeo.

When my mother found him in 1937 in Montréal he was a once, maybe twice-divorced furniture salesman. They broke up twenty-five years later in Pittsburgh over another woman. He was Romeo during the entirety of their marriage. I grew up in twenty cities in Canada and the US, among the sons and daughters of his women. A modern Romeo keeps a Monopoly set in the trunk of his car. 'You kids, play,' my father would say, and we did. I remember his face those days as he drove away: red, twisted, hideous as a bat's.

Their marriage began to end over a magazine article. In the AAA

Traveler he read a feature on San Miguel de Allende, a Mexican village of retired Americans drinking tequila by day, grilling steaks at night, keeping a ranchero with maids and cooks on pennies a day. He saw himself as Romeo Unbound in a frilly shirt and cummerbund on a hibiscus-strewn balcony, smoking in the twilight. At his side would be the musk-scented woman, lips of tabasco orange, glossy black hair pulled tight in a bun, bare shoulders with lots of cleavage showing. I was in the ninth grade and studying Spanish that year.

'Give me that book,' he said. He memorized the vocabulary in a weekend. My mother was not a Mexican type.

He went to Mexico with the last of his secret women, and married her at a resort that was owned by the sister of Ricardo Montalban. He met Ricardo Montalban one night and bought him a drink. After Mexico, he always bought Chryslers and walked like a matador. My father was a salesman, a gangster and a lover. He believed in charm and appearance and he was a charming, well-dressed man in public, nearly till the end.

That marriage in Mexico lasted about six months. That was 1961. She left him for a young Mexican with 5000 acres. My father sent me a picture from his hospital bed in San Miguel, a punched-out face, head in bandages. The death of Romeo. He married one more time, to a woman he met in Florida.

2. On our porch in Montréal one day in 1974 stood a young couple smoking Gauloises. He wore glasses with yellow lenses, wide-ribbed corduroy pants and a black leather bomber jacket. As I came to the door, he put an envelope back inside his jacket. The young woman – they both looked about twenty-two – wore a long, red vinyl coat belted with a silver buckle. Her jet-black hair was piled up high, gathered on top and allowed to fall like a tiny umbrella. It was absurd, but attractive. She was very pretty and Vietnamese, I guessed. Montréal was starting to receive thousands of Vietnamese. We lived pretty close to the l'Université de Montréal and I assumed they were a student couple looking for an apartment.

From the first 'bonjour' I knew he wasn't a Montréaler. He pronounced my name and I nodded. Then he said, 'I am Leo, your cousin from France. And this is my fiancée, Lorette.'

In my father's family, new cousins are always popping up. He'd been so much younger than the rest of his family that my aunts and uncles were infirm by the time I started getting curious, and then they were gone by the time I took a real interest.

'Cousin?' I said. He took it as a sign, and gave me a brief, back-thumping embrace. Lorette gave a kiss. My wife came downstairs and they fell back, astonished. She is from India. We were going out to some Indian function that night; she was wearing a sari and jewels.

'Uncle Leo told us you were beautiful,' said cousin Leo.

'And *asiatique*,' added Lorette.

The Uncle Leo referred to was, I realized, my father, then in Manchester, New Hampshire, with his fourth or perhaps fifth wife.

'He is very nice,' said Lorette. 'We saw him yesterday in Manchester and he sent his love.'

Mon-shess-taire. Her pretty mouth with the bright lipstick to match her coat, against her pale skin and black hair, made the name of that grimy mill town sound like a villa on the Mediterranean.

Our older boy came downstairs. He was nine, old enough to be curious about his family. He knew all his Indian relatives, their exact Bengali names with the proper suffixes and how they radiated from Calcutta to every part of India and the world. By the time he is ready to travel, there will be no major city in the world without his cousins. He knew all my mother's relatives, but he'd never met anyone from my father's side.

'This is your cousin Leo,' I said. 'From France. Leo, meet Leo.' Our son, too, was named for my father, although he has an Indian middle name. Like my father, he'll have to decide some time in the future how to travel in this world.

'A new country heard from,' said my boy.

'He's very handsome,' said Lorette. 'I wish Leo's father could see.' The world-wide gene pool at our son's disposal had served him well.

'I think I met your father,' I said. Young Cousin Leo's father was my true first cousin, son of my Uncle Bilou who'd gone off to war a Canadian and stayed to become a Frenchman. 'At your grand-father's – my uncle's.'

'I only saw *pépère* once. I was raised in Le Mans.'

'How is your father?'

'Ah,' said cousin Leo.

'He is against us. Like a crazy person,' said Lorette. She lit a new Gauloise. Our living room was already smelling like a *brasserie*. My wife went to get some wine.

'How can anyone be against you?' She was as beautiful as any woman in the world.

'You are enlightened, of course,' said cousin Leo. 'Unfortu-nately, my father is a fascist.' Fascist, if I remembered correctly, was an understatement.

'I wish his father was like your father,' said Lorette. '*What* a charming, sophisticated man! He showed us your wedding pictures. He showed us your books, the newspaper articles, he was *so* proud. He kept saying, "Just think, my little boy grew up to be famous and to marry a woman from *over there*. And you want to do the same." Oh,' she said, 'I was so proud to be part of your family.'

In those years, in Montréal, I had started to publish my books. For my father, who couldn't read them easily, holding them and showing them off to everybody was more than sufficient for us both.

Cousin Leo blushed. 'In a manner of speaking,' he said.

'In the eyes of God,' said Lorette.

'White or red?' asked my wife.

They both wanted Cokes.

'What is this called?' asked Lorette, reaching out and pinching the silk material.

'A sari,' my wife said. When I was Leo's age in Paris and meeting his father and my uncle for the first time, I had never seen an Arab, never seen a Vietnamese, and never seen an Indian woman. For myself, child of this French-speaking enclave on the shoulder of the New World, it was always difficult to reconcile old world innocence with our dreams of their corruption.

'My father has threatened to cut me off if I marry a foreigner. As if the Events of '68 hadn't happened.' said cousin Leo. 'That's why we saved our money and came to America. If we like it, we will stay.'

'Do you speak any English?' my wife asked.

'Not at all!' he boasted, lighting another cigarette.

'Would you like to stay with us awhile?' I asked.

'Lorette has a cousin in Montréal,' said Leo. 'Perhaps you know her, Nuyen Nhu? She can put us up.'

So another young man from my family was about to ensnare himself in Asia. The larger world impinges, finally, on every life, every village.

'We are not married – would that offend Madame?' he asked.

She bowed her head. 'Not at all.'

'Tonight we are in separate *foyers* of the université,' said Lorette.

'Is there anything we can do for you?' my wife asked.

'Yes,' he said. He took out a folded sheet of paper from the inside of his bomber jacket. It was a letter from my father, patriarch of all Leos in the family, to his aging nephew in Le Mans. Two halves of a divided family were meeting after sixty years, over this Asian woman in a red coat. Sometimes, like my wife, I can believe in everything mystical, in all the predestination and transmigration of souls.

'I told my father I will take Lorette around the world with me. I will get letters from every member of our families. I will even go to Vietnam and let them judge me. And I will give him these letters at the end and say he cannot be so stupid.'

He put the notebook paper in my hand. Then I read my father's letter.

My dear young Leo, child of my dear brother Bilou, my father had written, *I have met your boy and his beautiful young woman. They bring back to me the flavour of something lost. My own boy made a choice like your son and he has known happiness I have never known. It is not for fathers who provide so little to hold back so much. It is not for fathers to judge who their sons choose to love or even what they choose to love.*

'Isn't that beautiful?' said Lorette. I agreed that it was, the old fraud. I couldn't have said it better myself. I added as a postscript: *Leo, this is your cousin who pushed fruit with you, who drank with you,*

who saw you in your father's room and saw you in those other rooms. Do
not be a hypocrite. Passion alone will destroy all the barriers of this
world. We are only such things as our passion makes us.

3. In the winter of 1961 and most of 1962, I was working in Germany for the American Friends Service Committee. I'd just graduated from college. I had a toe-hold in Europe thanks to my
mother's German and my father's French, but it was literary
Europe that drove me, Mann and Céline especially. I'd turned down
graduate school. I thought it was still the twenties, or at a pinch the
post-war forties – art and existentialism everywhere. Travel and
language alone would fill me with stories.

The city they assigned me to was Wuppertal, famous in Germany for its *Schwebebahn*, the suspended railway that swings, hence
the name, down the middle of the Wupper valley. The train had run
unimpeded throughout the war. The only accident had been the
loss of an elephant that was strapped under a car while being trans-
ported to the zoo. The belt had broken, killing the beast and three
civilians on the street below. Old-timers in Wuppertal remembered
a famous bit of Nazi levity: the newsreel footage of a dead elephant
and the crushed civilians, then a cut to herds of elephants on the
African plains and the caption, 'Churchill's Secret Weapon?'

I was being billeted in a magnificent home high above the city on
the Wilhelms Höheweg by Frau Weiche, one of the women on the
board of the agency. My little room was on the third floor, under
sloping beams. The way to my room, up a narrow staircase not
much wider than my shoulders, was lined with drawings by Klee
and Arp. They were small and squiggly and unimpressively framed.
I nearly brushed them off the wall each time I went to bed. In the
grand salons on the first floor, the walls were ablaze with giant
Kokoschkas. Frau Weiche, as a young woman in Vienna, had been,
she said with a wink, Oskar's favourite model. Herr Weiche was
over eighty and rarely seen.

I read recently of the obscure glories of the *Wuppertaler*
Stadtsmuseum der modernische Kunst, well worth a day's side trip,
especially for their Klees, and the high-bourgeois Wilhelmite

architecture, and realized they were talking of my old Wuppertal home, now a gift to the city.

The greater world impinges on everyone.

On my job I was learning colloquial German, working with children and becoming reborn as a European. I was a *Mitglieder* in a *Nachbarschaftsheim* (how I loved to say the name!) on the Friedrich-Ebert-Platz in Wuppertal-Elberfeld and I would have stayed there, meaning Europe, forever, if I'd had money, or the offer had been made.

It was the time of the German Economic Miracle. Thousands of workers were pouring across the open border from the East every week, all of them with guaranteed jobs the moment they landed. I was in the middle of a revolution without knowing it. I was in Berlin when the Wall went up.

The agency that employed me ran a kind of day-care center for the *Schlüsselkinder*, the latchkey children of working parents. I took the kids on daily outings to the zoo and the swimming pools and sometimes just on day-long streetcar rides between the closely clustered industrial cities of the Ruhr.

Because Wuppertal was in the British zone of occupation, the young Germans I worked with were affecting British accents and reading P.G. Wodehouse. 'By Jove, ripping, old sport,' was a common response down in the laundryroom of the *Nachbarschaftsheim*, and the boys affected a wan and pimply air they confused with Upper Upper. The radio at the reception centre was tuned to the BBC European Service. It was the time of the Angry Young Men in Britain, with its eruption of working class and regional accents, which had disastrous effects on young Germans trying to learn the language with their customary thoroughness. My Pittsburgh English grated on their ears, though at least I had the passport of a British subject.

The most fulfilling job I could imagine would be to sit at the information booth in any large German city and handle all the travel inquiries, turning from German to French to Spanish to Italian to English without a break or an accent. I used to practise to myself. Having three of the languages down, and Spanish in a pinch, I thought only Italian blocked my path to perfect worldliness. I had the heart of a Common Marketeer. I wanted to remove the shame of provincialism from my soul.

The girl I was dating, which meant going to movies and sitting in parks, sipping beer with at a sidewalk cafe, had no use for England. She'd gone to Manchester as an *au pair* and found the British cheap and insulting. Her name was Hilde. She was a pale, broad, large-eyed girl with boyishly short blond hair and ruddy cheeks. I realize now she must have been a runaway, perhaps from the East or maybe a war orphan, though she never mentioned it. She said she was seventeen, but looked younger, and had been on her own since twelve. She wanted to go to America. She loved Americans. It was the Kennedy high noon, everyone was in love with America.

In the spring of 1962 on one of those German Catholic holidays that always took me by surprise – *Himmelfahrt* or Ascension Day – Hilde and I decided to go to Paris for the three-day weekend. My father was in Mexico at the Montalban resort, I was in Germany, my mother was back in Canada, and I had Uncle Bilou's address in Paris. '*Internationaler Playboy!*' Hilde joked, but she got us *Studenten Ausweisen* and cheap tickets on the chartered German Student train from Cologne to Paris.

Oh, father, I inwardly cried, look at your little boy now! The guitar-strumming Germans in their short pants and backpacks turned to me to lead them in 'Michael, Row the Boat Ashore,' and 'Hang Down Your Head, Tom Dooley.' How good they said my English was! I taught them fifties rock, American folk and show tunes. The stuff of my introverted fantasy life was converted suddenly to political statements, to sophistication. I was just like my father cutting a swath at parties with his professional voice and his repertoire of standard French songs in backwater places like Pittsburgh.

In Belgian cities our train with its special Deutsche Studenten Reisebüro logo got pelted with stones and eggs. The boys in our car cursed the cheeseheads in guttural mock-Flemish for refusing to sell us sandwiches and drinks through the lowered windows. They had no idea why they were hated. In France every open wall was smeared with slogans, 'Vive Bidault', 'A bas les arabes' and 'Vive la France/Vive de Gaulle'.

The stations were milling with young men in magenta berets and scratchy green uniforms, under blue clouds of Gauloise smoke. They were strapping, blond, farm and factory boys, too big for the French stereotype. We scrawny German pacifists sat inside, singing 'We Shall Overcome' and 'Blowin' in the Wind' with our super-strong Deutschmarks in our pockets while France tore itself apart outside our window. We pulled down our windows and serenaded the French soldiers with mocking little ditties praising Algerians and ending with *dix-huit mois en caserne*. The French boys responded with fists and upraised, bent-arm gestures.

Rue de Rennequin, off Place Wagram, is a fashionable street in an exclusive arrondissement near the Arc de Triomphe. My uncle's number corresponded to a six-story glass tower behind a high brick wall. The brass plaque outside listed the various architects' offices inside. Renault 3000s and the occasional Citroën were parked in the corporate slots, despite the holiday. The building was nearly all glass, and taller than anything around it.

The concierge's door was around back. The name outside matched my own, but for our Americanized spelling. From inside, I could hear the sloshing of water in pails.

There was no mistaking the man who answered. Shorter and far older than my father, heavier and coarser, he stood before me blank and sceptical, a Parisian with a thick, yellow cigarette butt in his lips. He was my father, back from some terrible future and still bearing the scars. That he could share so much of my father and be a stranger seemed a cosmic joke.

'I'm your nephew from Canada, Leo's boy,' I said. 'And this is my friend Hilde.'

He yielded the door, without a gesture. A major miracle to be admitted, when I think of the fifty years of separation, the movement across continents, the wars, the marriages.

'How is that boy?' he asked. 'Last time I saw him, he was nine years old.'

'In Mexico,' I said.

'Still married to Cécile?'

'I don't know any Cécile.'

He shrugged. 'So your mother's a Mexican?'

I told him my mother was back in Canada. At the time, I knew nothing of any previous marriages.

There was no electricity in the concierge's apartment of the Place Wagram Architects' Building. There was no floor, only loose boards over permanent puddles. I learned a lesson about the French soul that day, and the permanent relevance of Louis-Ferdinand Céline. An ice-chest drained into a grate over a permanent gutter, next to a standpipe of running water. He cooked on a two-burner campstove on a home-made table. A thickly built, moustached, grey-haired man was stooped over the standpipe, rinsing dishes.

'My boy, Leo,' said Uncle Bilou.

'I'm your cousin,' I announced. He sucked the information far back, nose first, then nodded. He was a short, wide, menacing man, with the dark blank face associated in French gangster films with Corsica or Marseilles. Hilde's French was very good; they guessed she was Swiss, or Alsatian. Leo told us he'd been a lifetime Army man, in the Resistance as a teen-ager, then Indochina, then Algeria. Demolition. Interrogation. Spoke Arabic like a pimp. He was a French patriot and now he was a man on the run without a country because the niggers had kicked him out of Algeria. Hilde spoke feelingly of a Zürich home. She too was a natural Common Marketeer.

'So, you want a job?' asked cousin Leo, after my uncle had poured us all some wine. I could not imagine a more inviting request, to work in Paris without papers. I was still plotting ways of staying in Europe the rest of my life. My patriotic cousin, wounded in Indochina, wounded in Algeria, needed help pushing a fruitcart which he'd had to bribe a Tunisian for. According to his vendor's licence his name was Mohammed Majoub.

Did we want to help him push? Tomorrow? Meet him here at three in the morning to be in Les Halles to select the fruit? To fight the Indochina and Algerian wars all over again? Okay, then. Finally he rose and gave me a big back-thumping welcome to the family.

Hilde and I were free in Paris for the rest of the day. We were observers of life, students of culture. Our clothes were German, so were my last two haircuts. We got into everything with our German student cards. Americans behind me grumbled, 'What's that card he's got? Look, she doesn't even shave her legs.' The greatest pleasure would have been to turn on them and say in perfect Pittsburghese, 'The 13:15 express for Amsterdam leaves on track 7; *le train direct d'Amsterdam de treize heures et quart départ de voie sept; Der Schnellzug nach Amsterdam von dreizehn Uhr-fünfzehn Minuten fährt aus Gleis sieben ab.*'

Evening found us exhausted on a bench in the Tuileries, wrapped in a sudden passion. It was April in Paris on a cool Saturday evening and all things were possible, except continuing the embrace at our student hostel, which was run by Valderee-Valderah Bavarian Catholics.

'Let's go back to your uncle's,' she whispered.

'What!'

'Come, it will be all right.'

We got back to Wagram at nine o'clock. We'd promised to be up at three for picking fruit. My request to Leo for a single sleeping space was treated as unexceptional. Cousin Leo kept military hours and fell into a loglike trance at nine-thirty, ten seconds after closing his eyes. My uncle was already asleep.

In moments of repose, as I tried to gather light enough to trace her outline, that fair, soft, boyish hair and the sudden immensity of her breasts, I thought it's not so bad, this first night of Parisian lovemaking, on a groundcloth over compacted clay in an unheated basement. Everyone should be so lucky. Hilde was a hefty elf by day, but at night became a veteran of Spanish beaches and Italian weekends, Christmases in Greece, not to mention piggish Britain.

Here, she'd say, you know how the Spanish boys do it? And in the total dark she'd guide me; and the Greeks, oh, the Greeks, such nasty things they do, she giggled, till I realized it was language I loved more than sex; the biggest thrill for me was the illusion of knowing something totally, loving a woman in her language. Everything else was invisible and unrepeatable. The language, I would remember forever.

Leo was strangely graceful and quiet in the dark, able to light the burners and make coffee for us all, then slice meats and bread into a pile of sandwiches for the day. Commando training. He had a small Deux-Chevaux, which got us to Les Halles, already bustling by four o'clock.

Mohammed Majoub was waiting at the prearranged spot, a dapper man in a blue smock, and we all shook hands in that crisp, solemn *copains de travail* ritual that opens every French working day. Leo really did speak Arabic, he transformed himself as he spoke. Hilde and I were given blue smocks. It took the three of us to push the giant, wooden-wheeled cart, even before it was loaded with apples, oranges, pears and peaches, tomatoes and eggplants. I loved it.

For a fascist, Leo had perverse attractions to certain parts of Paris. It was a cold, quiet Sunday morning on the cobbled streets around the Bourse. He wanted streetlife, he wanted the open bazaars he was accustomed to. As the blocks rolled by, the shop signs grew more to his liking; Arabic and Hebrew, and he was shouting his fruit-vendor's call, like a muezzin in the early sun. Hilde quickly learned the Arabic for each fruit and vegetable. I learned the prices. Leo stayed with us as we made our first few sales, to make sure we could work the handscales and not underprice, then took off his smock and left it draped over a mound of oranges. He unclipped his permit and stuffed it in his pocket. We could hear the night-shutters lifting in the coffee houses around us.

He shook our hands. 'It's all yours,' he said. He dashed off across the street and entered the darkened doorway between two shuttered shops. Upstairs, a light went on.

'He's got a woman!' Hilde remarked.

Eight hours later, after the wine and sandwiches, we were due back at the train station, and still no Leo. I put on the smock, took the money and went into the building, climbing the narrow stairs to the second floor. It was a different world: the cooking smells, the wailing Arab music, the children running underfoot. Clothes were drying in the hall. The building contained a small city, yet no one had entered or left it all day. Old men and women sat on stools, smoking, sipping tea and gazing indifferently at me. All the doors opened to the hall, with people of all ages and both sexes roaming at will. The men were unshaven, in undershirts and vests and baggy trousers. The women wore loose, bright skirts and layers of sweaters. They all looked like gypsies.

'Leo?' I called, figuring one more shout wouldn't matter. A toothless woman on a leather ottoman hissed and spat. '*Le fruitier, là-bas*,' I said, pointing to the street and making a pushing gesture.

She in turn shouted something croupy into an interior room. A male voice answered back. Young men appeared. I'd awakened a contingent of sleepy young warriors. Their French wasn't good, and I was afraid they'd mistake me for some kind of policeman. All the pleasant memories of Europe had vanished. Europe itself had vanished. If they were gypsies, the wad of bills in my smock-pocket made a frightening bulge.

Then Leo emerged. He was wearing a T-shirt and shorts. An olive-skinned woman stood behind him. He spoke in a loud, Arabic voice, and the boys scattered. He held out his hand to me, palm up, and I slapped the money on it. In Arabic he said something loud and joking, laughter came from all the rooms. In French he said to me, without winking but with ferocity so sincere I took it as overacting, *See how even the little Frenchmen have to pay me off? Say, here is your money, M Majoub. Say 'monsieur.' Say your cart is outside and I have sold all your fruit and here is your money.*'

I did as I was told. I thought, Passion, Leo, will dissolve the barriers of this world. Who can say whom we choose to love, or what we choose to love in another person? He patted me on the shoulder. Then he peeled off a few ten-franc notes and stuffed them in my pocket.

'Good boy,' he said. In Arabic he shouted something louder and everyone laughed. I took it as my *laisser-passer*.

'Now run along home.'

4. In 1964 I was in graduate school in Iowa City, married, nearly a father. Europe was still a pleasant memory, it always would be that, but merely pleasant, after marriage to Asia. My first Christmas back in the States, I'd sent Hilde a batch of American college catalogues. She sent me an art calendar for 1963: the work of Paul Klee, including two of the drawings in the stairwell we used that spring. She'd inscribed it with a line of Klee's: *Und wenn Du den Text nicht verstehst, so macht's nichts – die Bilder sprechen für sich* (And if you don't understand the text, it doesn't matter, the pictures speak for themselves). When the year was up, so were many of my tenderest memories of Europe.

The writer I would become was already being formed. University-trained. My European year was an aberration; I was a writer with an imperial, personal past. I was the czar of my childhood and adolescence.

My father was in Florida and married to his final wife after the drama in Mexico. My wife and I paid them a visit in Sarasota for Christmas. It's a vision of my father at his best.

He had a new Chrysler New Yorker. They had an air-conditioned house with a pool table, thanks to her money. The money looked like it would last forever, given the investments he was making. He took us on charter boats by day, and to different restaurants by night. Showing off the two new brides, he'd say, one a platinum blonde in her sixties, the other pregnant, in a sari. He busily learned a few Bengali phrases, he sang his French songs. It's a good thing they had money, because his new wife was helpless in the kitchen. She had to send out for broiled steaks and baked potatoes. When we got back to the house, unless I could interest him in pool, he'd sink into his usual funk and fall asleep.

'So, son,' he said. 'You're going to make me a grandfather.' That wasn't it, of course, but it edged us to the pit, the thing he'd been trying to tell me all his life. I'd never confronted him about Cécile. I wondered about other children.

'I've made a mess of things. But everything I've done I've paid for and I'm still paying for it, believe me. It's all evened out, except what I did to your mother. I feel bad about that. I always will.' He could tear up at will; tears were flowing now. 'Are you happy?'

'Very happy.'

'She's so different, son. I mean, she's wonderful, but she worships ... monkeys, things like that. I'm not saying it's wrong, but what will your children be? Do you think about that, ever?'

The answer could have been a simple no, but I wanted to end the conversation. I was fighting tears myself. 'It's not your place to ask. It's not your place to ask who I love or what I love or what I choose to love.' I thought suddenly of my cousin Leo, his inability to stop loving what he hated, or his need to love what hated him. 'Maybe I'll start worshipping monkeys. Don't try to be something now that you never were.'

It was the first angry word I'd ever expressed to my father, and like a scolded boy he quietly racked the balls and allowed me the break. After that, I became his father, as all children eventually do. For the rest of his life he treated me with deference.

The investments were all scams. So much of my father was shrewd and brilliant, but the rest was utter stupidity. Within a year they'd lost everything and he was back in Manchester, selling furniture. He worked till a heart attack in 1976, then phlebitis, and operations to restore circulation to his feet. We were living in Paris that year, when he and his wife visited us. I wheeled him around Montparnasse, and he held the Guide Michelin on his lap. I pushed him along as many streets as I had Leo's fruitcart fourteen years before. On a whim, we called young Leo in Le Mans, who had a radio shop. He was married, but not to the ravishing Lorette. They'd quarrelled and he thought she was somewhere in California.

My father's feet were white chunks of ice in constant pain. He'd refused to have them amputated. A year later, some feeling had been restored and he was planning to go back to work somewhere, selling furniture. He'd reached the age when he could work and keep all his social security benefits.

We were living in Toronto the day in late December, 1978, when he died. The doctor said he'd probably had a slight internal hemorrhage, the kind of thing everyone gets, but his anti-coagulant medicine had not been regulated in several weeks. In effect, he bled to death.

5. The cousins keep popping up. In the fall of 1987, we were invited to a big Sunday lunch at my cousin Justine's, in Brooklyn. We live in New York now, two official aliens. It is a move that seemed inevitable. We teach and write, our son is through college. There have been some major disappointments, but no serious disillusionment. I would still worship monkeys. In the way of these things, it is my wife's work that speaks to America. Mine is an acquired taste.

Justine is in her seventies, a true first cousin, what they would call in India a cousin-sister, the daughter of one of my father's many older sisters. It's her son, my age, a photographer and my first cousin once removed, who's become a friend. Justine's name had been given to me at my father's funeral by Corinne, a second cousin, appalled by my family ignorance. It's taken ten years for us to get together. And when I visit my cousin down in his Village apartment, he shows me more cousins, aunts, even my own *mémère* who died long before I was born. They're like galaxies, ever-receding, ever appearing, as more powerful detectors scan the void.

We're well into an Italian lunch – Justine married a Brooklyn Italian – her French is lost but not her memories of a Québec and Manchester childhood. It's a Bensonhurst apartment with crucifixes on every wall, and a plastic *sacré-coeur* on the credenza. She remembers my father, Uncle Leo, very well, on his trips down from Montréal and how her own mother used to warn her, when she was a teen-ager and he was in his middle twenties, not to be alone with him. He had a reputation.

'Deserved, I'm sure,' I say, my father now a peaceful memory, the psycho-magma somewhat cooled.

' "Always make sure Delia's there," that's what Mama used to say.'

'Delia?' I asked. 'Not Cécile?'

'Oh, my God, no. Cécile took the baby, you know, when he took up with Delia.'

'The baby?'

'Sure. What was his name? Strong little tyke, cute as he could be. He had a real Canadian name, and Cécile took him back up there. What was it, Joe, you remember?'

Her husband, quiet until then, frowned and closed his eyes. 'Romeo, wasn't it, Jussie?'

Meditations on Starch

POTATOES: Mr Spud opened at the local mall, and hired my high school boy for his first job. He was saving for a trip to Europe, where he has relatives.

He's been taught to do amazing things with potatoes. They're just a shell of their former selves. No longer prized for snowy yields, for understated contribution to stews, now they're just parka-like pockets waiting to be stuffed. It's the fate of blandness in the mall-managed world, I tell him, to be upscaled into glamour like pita bread and bagels, chicken and veal. Stuffed with yoghurt, sour cream and cottage cheese, spread with peppers, cheese and broccoli, topped with Thousand Islands dressing and bacon bits.

What wizard thought this up?

Mother!

I still like mashed potatoes. Even the name is honest and reassuring, after the *gepashket* concoctions with alfalfa sprouts and garbanzo beans. Butter-topped, cream-coloured bins of heroic self-indulgence, inviting a finger-dip the way a full can of white enamel compels a brush.

Is there a taste explosion in the world finer than the first lick of the Dairy Queen cone, the roughened vanilla from a freshly opened tub, the drowning in concentrated carbohydrate where fats and starches come together in snowy concupiscence?

CORN: My son never knew his grandmother, whose presence comes back to me as I stand at the Mr Spud toppings bar. She only exists in these sharpened moments, triggered by significant images that otherwise baffle me. 'Mother,' I murmur, 'what do you make of this?' Questions to my mother are questions to history, answers from her are brief parables of the twentieth century.

Don't you know? she tells me. The yearning for a clean, quick, anonymous bite is universal.

My mother found herself in Prague in 1933. Her art school in

27

Germany had just been closed down. One of her professors offered escape with him to Rio. Many went to Paris and Brussels. These weren't the Big-Time Bauhausers; New York and L.A. weren't in the cards. These were commercial designers ('but not designing enough,' my mother would joke). Shanghai, Istanbul, Alexandria, Stockholm, with the leaders taking off for Caracas and Rio. One got to Vera Cruz. Maybe eventually some of them made their way to America. My mother got to Montréal.

I was a stamp collector. I knew the tales behind those thick letters with the high-denomination stamps, the elegant handwriting in black ink turning to olive. Cancelled stamps are less valuable than mint, but I treasured them for the urgency of cancellation. My mother had known a time when the germ of genius was clustered in the back streets of Dresden and Weimar and Dessau, before the Big Bang flung it to tin shacks on the shores of Maracaibo.

The poles of her existence can move me to tears, the B. Traven world of artists from the heartland of order and austerity rotting in the rat-infested tropics. She showed me photos of an art college, hand-painted signs on a tin-roofed shack, Herr Professor in jodhpurs and bush shirt, teaching from a canvas deckchair.

'Poor old Dieter,' she'd say.

She'd wanted a career in fashion design. Her surviving portfolios from art school feature ice-skaters and ballerinas. She was the Degas of Dresden. But the faces of the skaters and dancers seem grafted on, dark and heavy, like hers. The eyes are shadowed, in the movie-fashion of the day. They stop just short of grotesquerie, for those girls will never soar, never leap. She could get the bodies, but not the faces. I can't tell if it's Expressionism, autobiography, or mild incompetence. I don't know if these were the drawings she kept out of fondness, or the ones that didn't sell. Others found their way into magazines. The idea of my mother influencing the Prague Spring Collection of 1934 fills me with wonder.

Or do I read too much into those drawings, too much into everything about her? Had she somehow, secretly, read Kafka? The idea of her Europe, of pre-war Central Europe, tugs at me, the continent I missed by the barest of margins.

There was no concept of Eastern or Western Europe in those days – Warsaw and Prague were as western as Paris. Russia and Spain, of course, didn't count; they were Asian, or African. Budapest and Bucharest had reputations for pervasive dishonesty, deriving perhaps from the perversity of their languages. So the stories I grew up with and passed on to my son were of an *idea* of Europe that hasn't existed in eighty years, a Holy Roman Empire in which a single language and a single passport dominated all others and the rest of the world suffered paroxysms of exclusion for not being European, and specifically, German.

When he was twelve, I asked my boy what he wanted to be when he grew up. 'A European,' he answered.

In Prague she got a job painting commercial signboards to hang over doorways, like British pub placards. One of the first signs she painted was for something called 'Indian Corn'. A corn café! Nothing but stubby ears of corn, cut in half, standing in pools of butter. In Prague, in 1933.

She had never eaten corn. Her parents considered it servants' food, part of a cuisine beneath serious cultivation. Nothing that required labour in the eating – and corn on the cob looked like work – was part of their diet. My grandparents, whom I of course never met, favoured pre-nouvelle cuisine French cooking, which meant soft, smothered, simmering things, the mashed potatoes of their day, short on fibre, low on spices, long on labour and quickly digested. Much favoured were compotes and warm puddings, since they detested anything cold as well as anything hot. Worst of all were the still-churning, molten messes that had become chic in Germany with the rise of Mussolini. Upscaling the lowly pasta. My grandfather's response to history is summarized in a single gastronomic grumble. 'Why couldn't *il Duce* have been a Frenchman! At least we would have eaten properly.' My grandmother, no less patrician, responded, 'Be grateful. He could have been Hungarian.'

Of all the stories I want to know, of all the things my mother told me of the secret lives of complicated people, I remember only these ridiculous little lines. So she painted her cob – half a cob, and the cobs weren't big in those days – standing up like a stubby candle in its pool of butter. Each kernel was treated like a window in an apartment tower, radiating a buttery light. It wasn't easy, before acrylics, before the conventions of Magic Realism, being a German artist, to devote herself to a humble corncob.

'I didn't know anything at first. Or maybe I discovered it as I worked. It was love for America,' is how she put it. 'A craving for Indian corn saved my life.'

Franz Kafka had been living a few blocks away just a decade earlier. He'd written *Amerika* under the same mysterious craving, though it didn't save his life. Maybe America-worship was in the air, at least among those who professed no longing for Germany. For my mother, Prague was just another provincial German city with an interesting Slavic component to be respected, but faintly pitied. She couldn't imagine civilized discourse in any language but German, with the possible exception of French in well-defined circumstances. French and German divided the dignified world between them, the spheres of pleasure and labour, though her French years were still in the future.

Her boss had a son, named Jürgen Jaeger – a good movie name, and he had dabbled in films like many German-speakers in the '20s. He still thought of himself as a set-designer, a property man ('but not a man of property,' he joked, and the joke has survived them all because my mother jotted it down). He also identified strongly with Hitler's Sudeten policy, feeling himself mightily abused by the majority Czechs with their dirty, mongrel ways. I am making him sound unappealing – a Hitler of sorts, another expansionist signpainter with acting ambitions, born on the rim of Germany – but my mother never did. His attitudes were too common to be evil. I'm sure most Prague-born German-speakers yearned for enosis with the Fatherland, all other implications of Hitler-rule to be put aside, temporarily.

This, then, was my mother's situation in 1933. She was thirty and unmarried, talented, attractive, and stateless. She had an admirer whose rechannelled ambition was to join the political and if necessary military services of the greater German state. I have seen his picture, the suggestive swagger, as I interpret it, of one leg up on the running board, elbow on the windshield, body tight against the touring-car's flank. No monocle, no duelling scars, but a leather coat, a self-regarding little blond moustache, and a short, elegant cigarette that can only be carried in a theatrical gold case. He strikes the pose of a big-game hunter, even on a Carpathian picnic in the summer of 1934. This is the man who must be eliminated before I can be born.

Pictures of my mother show her always smoking, though I never saw her smoke, nor empty an ashtray without a show of disgust.

I came into her papers five years ago. That's when I unwrapped the first of many portfolios she'd been keeping under her bed. I had never seen them, and she had shared everything with me, I'd thought, the only child, the late-born son, the artistic and sensitive man in the family. Some of these I had seen – my grandparents sometime in the late twenties at a resort in the mountains. Taking the Cure. All those faces, relaxing, carefree, getting away from business and the city and the nameless sickness that seemed to stalk them.

I look like my grandfather – her genes won out. The gene for baldness, carried through the mother. The gene for Alzheimer's disease – who carries that? My mother maintained a saving fiction all the years that she was able, that her parents could have left Germany in time, just as she had, there was an uncle in Montréal who would sponsor them all, but her father lost first the will, then the sense of all urgency. It was, in his case, a medical, not political problem.

'Who is this man?' I asked her, and she pretended to look, and to smile. 'He's very handsome, mama. Like a movie star.' Still no response. The photo is sepia, faded, and extremely small. If only it could be blown up, Jaeger and the touring-car, the mountains and forest in the background, I might understand just a little more. There are other pictures, equally small, taken from upper windows, overlooking city squares. Brno? Bratislava? Carlsbad? Prague, perhaps, or the view from Carpathian resort hotel. Maybe Jürgen is standing at her side, whispering, '*Sehr schön*'.

'Jürgen Jaeger, mama, does it mean anything?'

She held her hand out to appease me, her fingers now blue-edged tines, but she didn't look.

I can read German, speak it enough. Her old-style handwriting is difficult. *I tell him he must do what he must do. His father has interests in Germany. They have relatives in Leipzig.*

I read it out loud, looking at its author's face, which gives back nothing. She probably jotted down these notes in ten seconds, sixty years ago. Now, the simplest resurrected fact of her life embraces the world. If I don't take these boxes now, they will be lost. She is going away and won't be coming back, and we have decided we must leave Canada.

He says, 'Der Führer may be a little crude for your tastes, but he's no fool! He knows who makes money for him. And with this Rosenfeld getting elected in America, well....'

There is another tiny, sepia street scene. It is the most precious picture in the box. For an artist, my mother took terrible pictures. A tram snakes off the top of the frame. Half of a bundled Frau crosses the street. Uniformed men – police, army, Czech, German? – fill the space at the corner, outside a coffee shop. There seems to be an *Apothek* next door. Cold-looking children play a sidewalk game using chalk just outside its door. You would miss it if you weren't looking for it, the sign for *Korn* struggling for attention against much larger and fancier boards.

This is the picture to be enlarged, at any cost. I palm it and slip it away, knowing I am taking her soul, and fearing that something will slice through all the blown cells in her brain and reach out for it, and then destroy it.

Fly! Fly! Go west and don't stop. I tell you this as a friend, as someone who knows.

This on a worn sheet of airmail paper, initialled with what appears to be a double 'J' inside a crest, with a swastika hanging below it. So strange to see, as it were, a sincere swastika and not some gangland graffiti.

J.J., Visa Clerk, Leipzig.

RICE: In my wife's culture, Usha is called a 'cousin-sister' which means any female relative approximate in age. Actually she is Anu's first cousin, daughter of my father-in-law's oldest brother. In the ancestral long-ago, they had lived in the same Calcutta house, the *jethoo-bari*, part of a joint family numbering forty.

She is married to Pramod, and both are physicists. But instead of staying in the university world and settling down on some Big Ten campus, Pramod had taken a position in Holland, setting up a lab, and the Dutch government had recommended him for similar work in Indonesia and Surinam and before too many years, he had found himself side-tracked into sophisticated, high-level nuclear management, the protocols of which led, inevitably, to international agencies. He is now with the UN's nuclear-monitoring agency in Vienna, and Usha works as a researcher in physics for the University. They have been in Vienna for fifteen years, their children are European, they own an apartment in the city and a garden house in Wiener-Neustadt. It's a comfortable life in a country where immigration and assimilation as we know them are impossible.

We are all together this night in Vienna, enjoying a huge Bengali banquet, cooked from locally gathered fish and rice and vegetables, simmered in spices brought back from frequent trips to London and Bombay. My son and I have our Eurail passes, Anu will be with us only three days before going on to India to visit her mother and sister.

It's this life we lead, I silently explain to myself, and to the ghost of my mother. Vienna was another of her cities, briefly. The world has opened for us, no fears of the unknown. My mother shrank from the very idea of India, but tried to disguise it with images of Gandhi and respect for ancient wisdom.

How under-defined I feel, at fifty, compared to Pramod; a father who has written some books, who teaches when he must, who dabbles in cultures that have their hooks in him.

We are talking of Canada. 'They've become like the British,' Anu says, spooning out rice to our son. 'Hateful little people.'

The Sens had visited Niagara Falls last summer, and been turned away at the border for an afternoon's visit. For pleasure trips they use their Indian, not UN passports. 'He said things to us I wouldn't say to a servant,' says Usha Sen. ' "How do I know you will leave when you say? How do I know you own a house as you say?" They are very suspicious about Indians, I must say.'

'I told him to go to hell,' says Jyoti, the Harvard boy. 'Who needs the hassle? The Austrians are bad enough, but I always thought Canadians were better.'

I remember when it wasn't so, in our cosmopolitan refuge of Montréal, when my mother and I lived like Alexandrians in a large apartment in Outremont after my father's death. We had original paintings on our walls, French-Canadian artists only. My father was an old man even in my earliest memories, a lawyer nearing retirement, then dead two months after achieving it. I remember the visits of his grown-up children from an earlier marriage, of being the same age as his grandchildren, and of wondering what, exactly, to call our relationship. My son and Jyoti are, precisely, second cousins. Usha is his first-cousin-once-removed. He calls her *mashi*, aunt.

'Have more rice, please. There is plenty.'

'Mother, this isn't Calcutta,' says Tapati, the MIT daughter. Everything this evening is exquisite. There is no cuisine in the world that excites me like Indian, no painting that thrills me like Moghul miniatures, no city for better or worse, like Calcutta. After India, Europe is a bore. I'm staying back for my son's sake, his ancient dream of being European.

Anu is explaining our move to the States. 'To be Indian in Canada was to be a second-class citizen no matter how good you were, no matter how Canadian you tried to be. At least if we're second-class in the States we know it's because we're just second-rate.' I wish I could sink into the rice, the dimple-topped pyramids of snowy rice scooped out for fish and vegetables. I want to grab handfuls of rice and smear them over my head and rub them in my face. I want to do something vulgar and extravagant in this apartment of excellence, among these diligent and exquisite people, out of my own shame, the accumulated guilt and incomprehensions of my life.

Tapati is asking our son, 'Is there anything special you want to see in Vienna? I can take you there.'

They are amazed that for who he is and what he represents to them – America, after all, the place and people they most admire – he speaks only English. Usha's children have been raised in Europe, but with Indian ways. Each of them speaks eight languages, but they have no country. Jyoti writes rock lyrics in German, plays in an Austrian band, studies economics at Harvard. Tapati has a ph.d. and an mba and now interns at the World Bank. Both are in America, but not of it – too exquisite for the mall-culture America I know.

'Anything,' he says. 'It doesn't matter.'

'No, there must be something.'

He looks to me for help. He wants Europe, he wants saturation, a way of entering. He's been studying German in high school, but it's the last thing in the world he'll admit here to his second cousins. He doesn't trust himself to understand a single word. He's heard Bengali all his life, but never thought it part of himself. He spent half his life in a French-speaking city and did his French exercises perfectly, like history. It's the legacy of the New World. Jyoti has already told him, he'd trade it all – the languages, the sophistication that dazzles his Harvard friends – for a simple work permit, for the chance to stay and work the summer at Mr Spud.

'And what about you, Uncle?'

'Berggasse 19,' I say.

'The Freud house?' Usha asks. 'Why that – there's nothing there, believe me.'

'Wasn't he a coke-head?' my son asks in all seriousness, and the question sails over the heads of all but Jyoti, who smiles and nods. A conspiratorial friendship is starting to grow.

'Berggasse is very near my lab,' says Usha. 'We can take the tram there tomorrow. But it's not what you think – it's just a couple of rooms with photos on the walls.'

'Bor-ring,' Jyoti hums, as my boy suppresses a grin.

We're there at eleven o'clock the next morning, my son and I, and Jyoti who's brought his guitar along. He'll do Freud with us, and we'll do the music shops with him. He's promised us a tour of the lowlife dives of Vienna, the coffee shops where the Punkers hang out, the places where he spent his high school years avoiding expectations to be good and dutiful.

The first cousins have gone out for a proper Viennese lunch, *Kaffeeschlag mit Sachertorte*. Nothing that has to do with the man who once compared the ego – rational and altruistic – to Europe, and the libido – rapacious and murderous – to Asia, inspires my wife to sympathy. A foolish little man, racist and chauvinist, with bad science to justify it.

It is a sunny, summer day, cool but bright, sweater weather. Children are playing on the sidewalk of Berggasse, outside the corner *Apothek*. Jyoti says to us, 'Watch this – you think the Austrians know anything?' He asks the oldest boy, 'Do you know the Freud house?'

'Did they just move in?' he asks.

'Get that?' he laughs, turning to us. My son translates it.

'You could ask anyone on this street. Old, young, it doesn't matter. One group wants to forget, and the other one never knew.' We cross over the narrow street, looking for brass plates outside the formal doors. Number 19 is just a flat, as it always was, squeezed between other flats and offices.

Usha was right, it's only an old doctor's office cluttered with photos. The second-cousins browse respectfully, faintly embarrassed by all the fuss. It's all Jyoti can do not to unzip his guitar case and start banging out something scandalous for the Freud Museum. I don't know what I expected to find.

This is the room where all of them came, I want to say. Princess Marie sat there. And the young Viennese Circle – see their pictures! – met here, in this room. In this room, someone challenged the incomprehensible with bad science and bad politics, in the name nevertheless of reason. The smallest facts had the deepest gravity, chance events were all connected, public events were the ritualized form of private projection.

Son! Are you listening?

Someone dared to say our dreams had a pattern, our dysfunctions a cause, our beliefs a pathology. On the walls, the Holy Roman Empire surrenders, and Freud stands on the dais, Vienna's most honoured, most famous citizen, as the Austrian Republic is declared. Here, Freud is welcoming the President of the Republic and his cabinet on the quarter-century anniversary of *The Interpretation of Dreams*. His birth-cottage is decked with bunting.

And it chokes me, suddenly, the realization that science and music and literature can be so advanced, and do nothing to influence a political culture in its infancy. Austrian democracy was younger than Ghana's when the Nazis crushed it. I want to turn to my son and remind him of the great despairing poems I've read to him, of Yeats, of Auden, and the vast literature of the Holocaust that radiates from this room and a thousand others in this city, and echoes off these grey, sunny streets. The tradition, however faintly, I belong to. Poems about the imbalance of what we are capable of feeling and thinking, and what we have inflicted.

They've gone.

'They heard music outside,' the ticket-seller tells me. 'They said for you to follow the music.'

At first I hear nothing. I watch the children across the street, and the old women slogging their way from shop to shop, carrying groceries in string bags.

Berggasse slopes downward, and I follow it a block, half-imagining a rhythm, a few high notes and a beat in the air. Turn right, twist left. People are in the streets now, following something.

Up ahead in a small square at the rim of a fountain I can see them, clowns juggling, and a small crowd clustered. The performers wear top hats and putty noses, their cheeks are reddened, and one of the boys is darker than all the others, in a borrowed top hat, crouched on one knee like Chuck Berry, cutting in front of the clowns and drummers, leading everyone in lyrics I can't understand. And at the edge of the fountain is my boy in a borrowed vest and putty nose, punching a tambourine and doing a snake-dance on the fountain's edge.

Did, Had, Was

IT WAS A COOL, gusty Belgian morning, the low human landscape dwarfed by billowing clouds under a sky of porcelain blue. Over the Channel, a storm was brewing. Picard shivered; he'd been working out of Asia for nearly thirty years. He thought of the masters of the Flemish School and how innocently this commerce had begun: under the fluted clouds of grey and gold, the stubble of ships' spars in the distance, black-clad burghers in buckled hats unfurled their trading maps, while old empires crumbled and new ones rose. Ugly, slate-purple clouds were on their way. Pike's-eye purple, he used to call them when he fished for *doré* in Lac Mégantic.

He'd passed a northern childhood in the mountains east of Montréal. Weather like this, pinched summer days of the purest light and morning frost, had meant the end of summer and time of the apple-harvest. His father would hold the ladder, while his mother and sisters arranged bushel baskets under the trees. Gaby and Maty picked from the lower branches and tried to sneak windfalls into their baskets. At treetop level the spits of rain coming at him 'slantindicular', as his father called it, lashed his face and knuckles raw.

He remembered it sharply, being fifteen, standing in the mudroom just off the garage. Gaby with popcorn going in an old wire popper over an open fire, apple fragrance surging through the house from three hundred bushels stored in the garage for the second *presse* of autumn cider. And he would be waxing his skis for the winter's first run.

He had to remind himself that this was Bruges nearly forty years later. Rather than the train direct from Amsterdam to Paris, he'd taken this brief, nostalgic detour. He'd spent the previous night in Amsterdam with two Indonesian whores whose names he'd already forgotten.

Paul Picard, called 'the dean of Asian correspondents' had decided to retire. A school of journalism had wooed him with a major commitment: The Picard Centre of International Communications. A trifle grandiose for a man who'd worked alone for nearly half his life out of a two-room apartment with a portable typewriter, a notebook, and his remembered file of secret contacts.

He was on his way back to Canada, slowly. In the past eight months he'd interviewed leaders in every country from China to Turkey. Being Canadian, he was thought to be inoffensive and objective. He'd compiled a monumental file of tapes. Student assistants, a new and welcome concept, were already transcribing them.

The founding fathers of the Third World, the proud products of Paris and London, were already in place when he'd arrived in the late fifties. They had seen in him a mirror of their own impotent worldliness. He'd moved ever eastward, establishing contacts with a less savoury generation of emerging leaders while they were still deeply wedged in their military and civil services. He had an eye for talent. Over the years, his level of access had risen with them.

He'd opened China and reported during the Cultural Revolution despite eight months of house arrest.

He'd been the first witness to the slaughter of the Chinese in Jakarta, scene of his most widely anthologized piece, 'On the Streets of Jakarta, a Reporter Begs for His Life'. He planned to discuss it in his first public lecture in the fall. He would reveal it all: In Jakarta, a Reporter Is Caught in a Chinese Whore House. In Jakarta, a *Kris* Is Held to a Reporter's Scrotum until He Begs. In Jakarta he is forced to watch men, women and children being tortured and burned. It was, he felt, a paradigm of the reporter's art. Passion, contacts and luck into research and objectivity.

He'd covered the war in Bangladesh. And Vietnam. And Cambodia and India.

He'd personally carried diplomatic messages in Vietnam. He'd been barred from the United States.

He'd tracked the emergence of Japan and taken an early economic interest in Korea, Malaysia and Singapore.

He'd not neglected the arts and human interest, the film-makers, the painters, writers and traditional craftspeople. He'd lived with peasant farmers in India and Java, in China and the Philippines. He'd tracked a Thai physicist teaching quantum mechanics on a slate under a banyan tree. In thirty years he'd filed over 10,000 stories, 4000 in French, and written a dozen books.

He could walk into nearly any Asian capital and get an interview on short notice. Politicians have long memories; they owed him favours. He knew where their skeletons were buried. Since his next book would not be appearing for at least two years, an eternity in Third-World politics, normally guarded leaders had been generous with their time and revelations. *Adieu, Tiers Monde/Third World, Farewell* would be his autobiography, a reverse-Montesquieu laced with Henry Adams. It was in Asia that he came to understand the world, and where it began to elude him. His contacts were losing power, and dying. So was his memory.

One of his friends in Hong Kong used to joke, 'Picard, old man, the book you should be writing is the Erotic Atlas of Asia. Damned sight more useful.' There might have been a different woman for every story he'd filed. In a life that was otherwise monastic, women were his daily reward. Now that he was leaving the continent and its network of sexual convenience, he realized his dependence. On this final trip, he even found himself going to prostitutes before his interviews. It was a challenge. In the Ayatollah's Iran he'd found women within sight of the central Mosque, despite the threats of death by stoning.

In Bruges, he was remembering a town of almost perfect proportions. It seemed to him it must have been Bruges where he'd gone up from Paris to meet Daisy Lesser on one of her trips from Boston, and they'd had three days of walks and bicycling, perfect food and long conversations that had settled them in their lives. He'd just broken up with his girlfriend of two years. Daisy had grown tired of Harvard Square and decided to settle in Israel. He'd had one of his bad migraines and he remembered Daisy sitting with him and reading in his room as he tried to sleep it off and from that moment he realized how good a person she was. Some sort of higher friendship was possible between young men and women. He associated it all with Bruges and its perfect light.

The Bruges he remembered was a town glazed in highlights, brick homes with glistening doors and shutters, each brick pointed precisely, every leaf of every tree etched against a cloudless sky. The effect, like a Magritte, was surrealist in its perfection. *Ceci n'est pas une pipe.* He remembered the geese and swans, fish restaurants and the nutty sweetness of Belgian crepes. Even now he could conjure the lemony smell of tiny Belgian potatoes roasted in parsley butter. He remembered the peculiar green squiggles of goose droppings on the walking path, precisely the streaked colour of weathered copper, and he was back to his student days at McGill when all of Montréal was low and grey, with green streaked roofs. He remembered a passionate young couple at the table next to him discussing fine points in Thomas Mann. Only in Calcutta and Bruges did people care so much for books.

One of the agonies of spilling too much of one's life in the Orient, and learning to adjust to it, is to render Europe as too angular, too orderly. Civic neatness no longer inspired him. Bruges, this cold June morning, was cheap and vulgar. He spent a numbed morning walking along the dikes but feeling pushed out by the German tourist buses. He reboarded the first train for Brussels to pick up his bags and connect with the Paris express.

He was aware, from time to time, of his own faltering mind. He found himself all too frequently unable to finish a sentence, losing the clear conclusion before he could get there. He indulged the need to interrupt, for fear he wouldn't remember his own response. He remembered his mother in the years before her forced retirement. What he and his father had taken as irascibility, then paranoia, proved to be mental bankruptcy.

'No more deposits, no more withdrawals,' his father had said, tapping his head while his mother stared in space. They sold their newspapers and went to Florida.

Now, for Picard, the perfect words were refusing to yield themselves. He could picture – almost smell and almost hear – the word he wanted. He knew it by syllables, by first letter, but it would bury itself deeper in the folds of language whenever he tried to pull it out. Words were like the fat sluggish mountain carp that lolled at the end of their dock back in Lac Mégantic. Huge things that wouldn't take a hook, that wouldn't flinch even as he dived in above them, and would only twist away when he sounded their depth and tried to spear them.

You could catch them when they spawned. They thrashed around like otters in the shallow water.

He had to keep consulting the notes he'd made to himself: his suitcase receipt at the *consigne* in the Bruxelles-Nord station, the address, phone number and directions to Daisy Lesser's house far out in the Paris suburbs. Parisian addresses had been so easy, when he'd last lived there thirty years before. No one considered living outside the city gates. Rueil-Malmaison sounded like an address in New Jersey or Long Island, or parts of Montréal that had become chic in his absence.

He plodded through the Gare du Nord, as instructed by Daisy's letter, then caught a suburban train to downtown Rueil, then the Malmaison bus. He stood in a shelter with half a dozen Down's syndrome labourers, short, thick, profane men in caps and blue smocks, smoking their foul yellow cigarettes and carrying their lunch pails and rolled-up papers. It took him a while to understand their French, but it seemed they were talking about an American singer named Madonna.

2. To Picard's father, a self-defined 'Darwinian Catholic' and old-fashioned patriot, Canada was a genetic blunder. Man's biological imperatives were clearly thwarted by life in the sub-tundra. This explained Canada's lack of true accomplishment in the arts and sciences. *Homo sapiens* (his father invested his generalizations with ponderous Latinisms and obvious chemical formulae) was a creature of the savannahs. He stood peltless and erect. Catholic man, however (which was to say, moral man, enlightened man), does not

abort his blunders. There was only one compelling reason for ever leaving Canada to go to the United States. The word was warmth; it took the shape of Florida.

A hundred miles east of Montréal, the family names and home-languages were thoroughly confused. Hence his parents: Alastair Picard and Fabienne Dussault Meacham. For years, Picard Senior's paper, *Herald of the East*, and its French-language counterpart published by his wife, *L'Herald de l'est*, lamented Canada's 1949 annexation of Newfoundland. Imaginative negotiators should have picked up Barbados – a warm-weather port – instead. Readers of his mother's paper were invited to plaster the French West Indian islands of Martinique and Guadaloupe with referendum ballots to join Canada, clipped from the French edition. The French government eventually protested.

One other reason for leaving Canada was tolerated in the Picard house. Call it access to culture or education. A winter in New York, timed to the concert season, was not disgraceful. Neither was education if it went by the name of Harvard, Yale or Princeton.

He'd tried for the Ivy League coming out of boarding school, but failed. He'd gone to McGill, done well in English, classics and hockey, and edited the *Daily*. Life in Montréal in the mid-fifties was claustrophobic, relieved only by the presence of Leonard Cohen, the cheap bistros of the east end, and the coffee houses opened by the Hungarian refugees. Cold cherry soup was the very elixir of worldliness. All of Canada's writers lived in London or Paris.

Montréal's undeniable attraction was its complicated linguistic etiquette. For those who'd mastered it, or been born to it, every other city on the continent seemed simplistic. He graduated in 1958 and told his father he was off to Harvard for graduate school. Radcliffe ran a celebrated summer course in book-editing and publishing. He planned to get hired in Boston or New York, and become a famous editor. His great desire, then and always, was to be a Maxwell Perkins, a discoverer of talent.

He had some advantages over his editing classmates. He'd been raised with the French and British classics. Thanks to a boarding school that taught Latin and Greek, a home life that included French, a father who carried a copy-editor's special pedantry into every conversation, and a McGill arts curriculum that modelled itself on Oxford, he was far better educated than most Americans. He could spell, write fluently, and was sceptical where most Americans seemed enthusiastic by birthright. He was the only male in the class (in that distant, pre-feminist era) who'd read Virginia Woolf.

He remembered walking down Brattle Street that summer and feeling mildly envious of a typical Harvard Square product – a young man in work shirt and blue jeans, tweed jacket and tie – who was at that moment passing on his Lambretta scooter. He made a sudden U-turn and called out, 'Daisy!' so enthusiastically that Picard himself had turned, and stared in the face of Daisy Lesser, a woman from his editing class.

Until that moment, she'd seemed to him a perfect editor, quiet and studious with long earrings, lean and pale with thick black hair and large blue eyes behind black-rimmed glasses. The thought that she had friends like the man on the scooter, that she had a life at all beyond books, changed his perceptions immediately. She wasn't pale and retiring; she was witty and forward. 'Daisy' wasn't just a sunny name from mountain fields of grass and flowers; it was also slightly corrupt, like Daisy Miller and Daisy Buchanan. He wanted Daisys to stay Daisy-like – old-fashioned and smelling of salt spray and apple cider.

She recognized him, tapped him on the shoulder and said, 'Let's have coffee some day,' then ran over to the man on the scooter and hopped on the back.

Picard felt he was, momentarily, in Europe. It seemed Parisian, and for some strange reason, the memory of that moment condensed his future as well as his past. Daisy Lesser entered his life that day to become an emblem of his first freedom in Boston, and it seemed inevitable, once he got to know her, that their lives would run in rough parallel. She came to symbolize the life of Harvard Square in the late fifties: living arrangements out of *Jules and Jim*, in unheated apartments with the gas ovens on and blankets over the

45

window; despite the poverty, frequent parties with crisp bread and red wine, pasta dinners that lingered in the memory as somehow perfect.

He thought of the scooter of Harvard Yard as a reaching out for Paris and Rome. Scooters were a pledge to trust and intimacy, a denial of the armored and efficient American self. He'd had a scooter in his first year in Greenwich Village, but sold it when he moved uptown.

By then he was a very junior editor in the text acquisition department of a textbook publisher. He was involved with a woman in Boston – not Daisy, who'd gotten a job editing a Harvard physics publication. His girlfriend was a McGill classmate, now a resident internist at Mass Gen. Once in a while he'd call Daisy, catch up on gossip about their classmates and then, discreetly, about her current loves. She had the nearest thing to a Continental existence of anyone he'd ever met.

Marriage was on his mind, except that Mindy had applied for a two-year post-doc residency at the Pasteur Institute in tropical medicine. There were no jobs for junior text acquisition editors in Paris. He spoke to a friend at the *Times*. There was a chance, he said, if he took a cut even from his measly editorial salary, to get assigned to the Paris bureau for a couple of years, given his skills in the language. The work could be laborious, but the Paris setting might make up for it. For forty-two dollars a week, he took it.

After a year in Paris, Mindy was sent by the Pasteur to Madagascar, of all places, to study the transfer of certain viruses from lemurs, to monkeys, to humans. He applied for press credentials, in hope of writing it up.

Within two months, he had made contact with cells of communist guerrillas. He interviewed grizzled old French *colons* with attitudes that would have been reactionary even in Algeria. He found an outpost of Indonesian linguists, attempting to draw a linguistic map of Madagascar in hopes of finding the precise landfall of Indonesian mariners, and to match it with the precise point of departure from the Indonesian Archipelago. He heard the unmis-

DID, HAD, WAS

takable accents of his own ancestral French and discovered that
Catholic education on the island was historically the responsibility
of Sacré-Coeur Fathers from Québec.

By the time Mindy went back to Paris, it was too late for Picard.
He'd committed himself to instability, an article a day on a world
around him that no one had ever seen before.

Mindy went back to Canada. Picard found a room on the Vau-
girard in Montparnasse, a property that corresponded, accurately in
those years, to Connecticut Avenue on the French Monopoly board.
By then, he'd discovered the intoxication of a journalist's freedom:
to lay out a new course of study every day; to turn from medicine to
politics to film-making in a single week, to see a dozen articles taking shape, like auto bodies on an assembly line. Here, only the
windshield wiper blades are missing. There, the bumpers, the
doors, and far off, years away, the engines.

3. Daisy Lesser owed her married name, Famahaly, to her brief
career as a physics editor, and to Picard's even shorter stay in
Madagascar. She had gone to Israel for a few months but found it as
loud and grating as Harvard Square. She'd shown up one day in
Paris, calling him from Orly and wondering if she could stay a while
to sort out her life.

Most of his Paris friends were radical *malgache* students at the
Sorbonne. His closest friend was Louis Famahaly, a physics post-
doc, Marxist pamphleteer and poet. Picard introduced them, and
overnight Louis went from left-bank *poète maudit* revolutionary to
pipe-smoking, wine-sipping Paris sophisticate. They were married
before Picard left for Beirut and the beginning of his Asian career.

Only the Americans do suburbs well; only Americans believe suburbs to be a profound good. For everyone else, especially Euro-
peans, suburbs are a consolation – and they look it – for not being
able to afford a city. By the time Picard found Daisy's house on rue
Emile-Augier, it was dark and cold and the Belgian rain had spread
throughout the north of France. The houses were tiny, with the

lawn area sacrificed for parking space. The last house on the street was Daisy Famahaly's. Characteristically, she was standing by the opened door.

'Only eight hours late, Picard. The soufflé has fallen. I've drunk the wine.' If anything, she was thinner than ever. No grey in her hair, and nearly his height. They embraced at the door, she led him inside.

'I went to Bruges,' he said. She poured them both some wine.

'Bruges,' she snorted. 'Whatever possessed you?'

'Was I wrong to remember it fondly?' He wanted to say: I needed clarity and perspective. I wanted to possess the perfect modesty of Bruges for just an hour or two.

They were sitting in armchairs in the *coin malgache*, under bright batiks and mounted funerary sculptures from a Madagascar grave. Louis was at CERN for the summer, accelerating particles. The son, Clovis, was in Boston visiting her parents. Siri, the daughter, was in Madagascar, visiting his. Daisy had settled into a career of writing: stories and poems and occasional reviews for British and American magazines. Twenty-eight years in France; what a strange set of classmates they'd become. She felt as strange in America as he did in Canada.

'That's right, Bruges used to be very pretty. Then the Germans and British discovered it. And we were there, weren't we? And you got sick somehow, I remember that.'

He tapped his head. 'Migraine. I don't get them any more.' He knocked on the wooden chair-arm. Now, just as frequently, he got the dancing lights and foreshortening, the whole migraine aura without the headache's following. One of the hidden benefits of ageing.

'You and your poor head. I remember sitting with you in Boston. Your hands got cold and you asked me to hold them and I thought, 'This is very novel.' But they were cold, so I made you some tea to hold. I used to ask myself: How is this man going to survive in the world?' She dropped her voice to a whisper. 'Would you like some tea now? Decaff?'

He was starting to feel uneasy.

'What I remember about Bruges,' she went on, 'is us sitting in some little restaurant having this very loud debate about the virtues of Thomas Mann. I was for him and you were against. You had these very set opinions about literature. It was all Flaubert and Balzac and Dickens and Thackeray. I liked the Russians and the Germans and even some of the Americans which you, of course, had never read.'

'I hadn't remembered. But I remember your sitting with me in Bruges when I had a headache.'

'Maybe so. You've had a lot of headaches. You've probably had headaches and someone to sit with you in every city in the world.'

She wanted to know about this deanship business, of which she strongly disapproved.

'I felt it was time. They told me what I knew and what I could pull in was worth a six-storey building with my name in marble.'

'Picard, what you know – even what you've forgotten – more than fills a six-storey library.' He kept quiet.

'But I feel mentally old,' he finally admitted. She turned on the late television news. 'Who doesn't? Especially you. You're probably burned out from trying to understand the Japanese or whatever.'

It's what they all said. He'd gone to a doctor in Tokyo who prescribed more exercise and contemplation, then marriage to a simple young woman. After a certain age, chaos becomes exponential in a man's life and the brain rebels. Picard had thought the diagnosis excessively Zen. It was easy to admit that Picard looked and sounded tired; being *seriously* impaired was inadmissible.

'There's lots of American news these days. I like to get the French slant,' she said. She used it in her stories.

It seemed that the chief US spy, a decrepit old man by the name of William Casey, had just been diagnosed with brain cancer. He'd had a seizure on his way to testify. The French arrange these things a little less obviously. Picard knew nothing of the case, which appeared to be about arms trading with the Ayatollah. It was practically impossible to understand how Americans operated in the world. From time to time over the years, Picard had asked American journalists about each new president, and gotten such grotesque responses he'd tried to ignore them. America was increasingly inscrutable to him.

'Listen, can you make out what they're saying?' she asked. The original American soundtrack was barely audible, under the running French translation. 'They don't know how to refer to him! "He was ... is, I mean ... He did, I mean does" ... that's really weird. Did, had, was.... Does, has, is.' She scribbled it down on a scrap of paper. 'I can use that,' she said.

He woke up in the night in a room so dark he thought his eyes were closed, and couldn't be opened. The girl was close tonight, as she often was. Suhan. Fifteen, she'd said. He'd been with her three times, a violation of his own principles, such as they were. All because he'd seen her one day holding on to a boy on the back of a scooter, and the boy had looked to Picard like a student, or at least studious, and that didn't tie in with him giving rides to very young whores.

There had been rumours for weeks of Mao's involvement in Indonesian politics, his influence over Indonesian communists. That night, he'd wandered through Suhan's place of employment. In a back room he'd paused in front of a coir curtain and seen the same young man again, drinking beer with friends. On the wall behind them was something Picard should not have seen – a portrait of Mao Tse-Tung.

Suddenly, things were clear, though hardly publishable. The whorehouses of Chinatown had been politicized. The Chinese of Jakarta were Maoist. That's when Suhan had been sent out to turn him away, and he'd been willing to be turned, like never before. She'd come out of the back room and stood in the dingy hall. Unlike every other woman in the house, she was dressed in sandals and a pleated skirt and a white cotton man's shirt buttoned to the throat. She simply raised her arms high and ran her fingers through her hair, and as her arms rose up, so did the untucked blouse, merely to the midriff and the lower line of her bra. In a continent like Asia and a city like Jakarta at the time of its most wretched crowding and ethnic violence, such sights were replicated on every corner. But

Picard had followed her and in this nightmare he was still following her, after twenty-three years.

She'd gone from precocious confidence in all her charms, the smile of calm, perfected wickedness, to the universal innocence of her death in a matter, perhaps, of several seconds. In the nightmare, the two masks of her face were reversed, and he'd followed the death mask down the hall and confronted her sexiness in the moment of death. He felt like her murderer.

There'd been scrambling in the hall. The building was too flimsy for the noise of broken glass or splintering wood. There'd simply been Indonesian boys going from room to room with revolvers and machetes and Picard had grabbed Suhan's hand and she'd taken his shirt to put over herself. They headed for a back door, he pushed against it and they'd suddenly been outside in a screaming, fiery night. His car with its PRESS sticker was near and as they ran towards it he felt a lightening of her grip. He turned then and saw her arm fall from her body in one machete blow by a child younger than she, a boy wearing a T-shirt with an American sports team logo and a red headband.

It's the look on her face that only Picard has seen. It must be the look reserved for the executioner by the condemned. In her face he saw every woman he'd ever lusted after, every face he'd ever loved. She had only a split second to look at her stump of an elbow and then to look at the boy who brought the blade down across her face.

'You were shouting,' said Daisy, as she turned on the hall light. He was in a teen-age girl's room with its Parisian maps and trophies, its school books.

Daisy was holding a glass of water. He could see the white roots of her hair, dry, puffy skin. She felt his forehead, and he realized he was shivering, though not from fever.

'What's really the matter?' she asked.

He remembered an old journalist he'd known in Calcutta. One day he'd come shivering into Picard's hotel room. He'd seen two tram cars linked together. Their four-digit identification numbers were those of his birth, 1918, and the current year. Picard had tried to reassure him that not everyone in Calcutta born in 1918 who saw that tram was going to die that night, that some emblems have to be mere coincidence.

'I'm living in the past,' he told Daisy.

'Bullshit, Picard.'

'My brain is sick. It's dying.'

'I said bullshit. You're our Orwell. If anything's wrong it's bad food and no rest and probably a lot of bought sex. You're worse than Louis. Watch out for that kind of stuff in the West, with AIDS.'

Another word he'd encountered in the American press, but hadn't bothered to understand. It hadn't penetrated Asia.

'Find a good woman back there in Canada who understands your work and let her help you. Don't be like the Trinidadians say, a "mutton playin' lamb." You're a mutton now, Picard, so take better care of yourself.'

He remembered driving his mother around North Hollywood, Florida, in the years after they'd retired. One day she'd turned to him and said, 'I know you're very familiar and I'm sure we've met.' She'd been sixty-two years old.

'All those tapes I've sent back – they're bullshit,' he said. 'I don't know these guys any more. I try to make out questions in advance and I end up looking for women instead.'

She gave him a European sleeping pill, something that knocked him out gently and dreamlessly. When he woke in the morning, he saw she'd left a nightlight on.

4. Mornings were his best time, especially the cool, wet mornings of Paris, life in the crisper-drawer, preserving every leaf and fruit, settling the dust, focusing the light through millions of tiny filters. The pill had left no side effects; he was downstairs by seven, alert and rested, and rummaging through the kitchen to find the coffee beans. He ground them up in an old hand held *moulin*. He thought he'd surprise her with coffee and baguettes on a tray. By the time the coffee had brewed, Daisy burst in through the kitchen door in light gloves and a running outfit. She pulled off her sweatband and gave

him a light, solemn kiss, the way French workers shake hands each morning.

'Better?' she asked.

'Much.' No one would think they'd been classmates: he was bald on top, grey on the sides, sallow-skinned and deeply wrinkled. A candidate for skin cancer, the young reporters always said. They had notions about hats and sunscreen. She had the hair and skin of a college girl.

'I don't suppose you run, do you, Picard?' He'd been astonished by the presence of runners in Hong Kong. He'd even seen them now in India. In Japan, of course, it was a rage. 'Everyone our age in the West is into running. Do it, the circulation is good for the brain.'

'The people I see running look like they don't need it. The people I see drinking diet colas look like it doesn't make any difference. From that I've concluded to lay off diet soft drinks.'

'I run three miles every morning. You can join me. I run for mental health, not physical.'

'I couldn't run fifty feet,' he said.

They each had business in Paris; he with the editors at AFP – he was hoping to arrange summer internships in future years for some of his bilingual students – and she to browse the English bookstores, the galleries, then take care of a hair appointment. There was a cousin of Louis's she was meeting for lunch. She and Picard would go into the city together on the bus and train and Metro, then arrange a time and place for dinner.

She was planning a book on Madagascar, on the clash of Africa and Asia on a single island, in a single people. 'The Incredible Shrinking Island,' she called it, a culture the world had managed to mislay. The French Foreign Office had the necessary documenta-tion, and she was probably the best-connected foreigner in the world, to tell the story. What India was to the British, Madagascar was to the French.

'A sobering thought,' he said. He remembered the imitation

Parisian culture of Tananarive nearly thirty years before: sidewalk cafés, baguettes delivered in Renault vans, potable red wines and the most arrogant prostitutes outside of Sweden. To the French, a successful colonial enterprise.

He extracted a meaningless promise from the managing director of Agence France Presse to of course consider M Picard's personally recommended students, since it would cost them nothing. He dropped in on the editors at Hachette who'd brought out two of his books, and assured them that *Adieu, Tiers Monde* was proceeding valiantly to a provocative conclusion sure to win him a spot on 'Apostrophes.' He spent several hours trying to find his favourite old museums, only to learn that modern paintings now hung in a loud architectural monstrosity known as the Pompidou Centre and that the Expressionists had been moved from L'Orangerie. He ended up communing with the Egyptian sarcophagi in the Louvre until it was time to meet Daisy for drinks at a bistro of her choosing, near the East African library of the Sorbonne.

He wanted to say, like Freud of America, it is all a mistake. This modern Paris, his life. He'd passed women during the day, especially a Vietnamese girl, obviously available, who would have given him the only calm he trusted. It would be unfair to say of Daisy she was twittering, but it sounded to him the way French women often sounded, only she was speaking English, bouncing from topic to topic like a mind on drugs. The bistro was loud and densely smoky. He wanted a dark, quiet room, moments alone and chance to focus on just one thing.

'The restaurant is just around here,' she said, as they stepped out into a cool, moist evening, for which he was grateful. 'There's a lovely *lyonnais* place, simple country food that Louis and I adore –'

He knew this area, knew it intimately. He'd walked these streets for years and it brought him some moment of peace now, to be walking these streets with a woman, her arm lightly in his.

'There's a marvellous Hungarian place,' he said, 'just down that street. Basement, cheap, great cold cherry soup. You like cold cherry soup?'

'Of course. I didn't know you knew –'

'Know this place?' He turned around, getting his bearings one last time. The grey bulk of the university buildings, the narrow streets clogged with students, the cool air of a summer night in the northern latitudes. 'Of course I know it, didn't I go to McGill for four years?'

He felt one last tug from her arm, her touch on his shoulder. 'Picard,' she said. 'Whatever you say.'

Dunkelblau

WILLI NADEAU has lain abed since birth, dumb and apparently unreachable, his bones as fragile as rods of hollow glass. He sleeps on pillows, his crib is padded. He is four. His mother is forty-two and has lost her only family. The boy, the lump, is all she lives for. Two succeeding pregnancies have ended in the seventh month. She remembers a burning, the heavy settling, and knows she is carrying another death. A brother is still-born and a sister, lumpish as Willi, survives three months. Willi lives – if that's the word – because he is the first, before she developed antibodies to his father. His parents are profoundly incompatible.

In 1944, Army research synthesizes a thyroid extract. The pills are tiny, mottled brown. Two weeks after giving him the medicine, his mother feels his neck twitch as she sponges him in the kitchen sink. A week later, he kicks, and in a moment as dramatic in his family as Helen Keller at the water-pump, he starts singing the words and music of 'Don't Fence Me In'. He justifies all her faith in keeping him at home, in reading the medical journals and pestering doctors, the four years of talking to him in both her languages, reading to him, hanging maps and showing pictures.

Like many a genius before him, though he is nearly five, he speaks in complete sentences before taking his first step. He demands his dozen glasses of cold milk a day be served in a heated bunny mug. He is a wilful, confident child, his mother's image. He likes the feel of heat on his lips, the icy cold going down. Each glass has to have a spoonful of molasses or of Horlick's Malted Milk, unstirred, at the bottom. No flecks of cream can show. The nightly slabs of liver or other organ meats, purchased on special rations, are shaped into states or countries, pre-determined by Willi and his mother from prior consultation. She starts taking him to Carnegie Library and Museum as soon as he can walk.

He memorizes the Pittsburgh trolley-numbering system. The Holy Roman Emperors, the Popes, the Kings of England. He memorizes everything, his brain is ruthlessly absorptive, a sponge, like his bones and muscles. Toy-sized yellow and red trolleys pass across a forested valley outside his bedroom window. He is still unsteady on his feet in the winter of 1945 when they take their Number Ten trolley down to Liberty Avenue and then one of the Seventies out to Oakland to the Library and Museum.

His first memories are of the Library, the smell of old books, the low chairs and tables of the children's room, and of staring into the adult reading room – no children allowed – while his mother checks the carts of new arrivals. The adult room is a cave of wonders, where steam rises from the piled-up coats and scarves. The six-storeyed ceiling, the polished wood and the corridors of books overhead absorb the coughs and page-shufflings of the white-haired men and women who sit around the tables. That is the world that awaits him – admission to the adult room, permission to sit under those long-necked lamps that hang from the rafters six floors up to nearly graze the tabletops, flooding the tables with a rich yellow light under bright green shades. It is a world worth waiting for, like the dark blue volumes of *My Book House* which his mother reads from every night and which are laid out above his bed, mint green to marine blue, a band of promise to take him from infancy to adolescence.

The main hall that connects the Library with the Museum is lined with paintings that his mother holds him up to see. Murky oils, Pittsburgh scenes from the Gilded Age, opera-goers alighting from horse-drawn cabs in the gaslit snows of Grant Street, children riding their high-wheeled bicycles down Centre Avenue. He feels the stab of every passing, irretrievable image. He can look in those faces of 1870, at the girls with their hands in fur muffs and their collars up, their eyes glittering and cheeks round and pink and full of life, and know exactly what his mother is thinking, because she is always thinking it: even these happy children are all gone, as dead as the snows and horses and all but the finest buildings, gone forever.

And there are darker Pittsburgh landscapes, with the orange glow of hellish pits fanning through the falling snow, the play of fires lighting the genteel ridges high above. Pittsburgh, with its blackened skies and acrid fumes, its intimate verticality of heaven and hell, forces allegory on all who live there. 'So simplistic,' she says, drawing his finger so close to the canvas that the guards stand and snap their fingers. Columned mansions on gaslit streets, perched above the unbanked fires, the bright pouring of molten streams of steel by sooty, sweating men far below. Heaven and Hell on the Monongahela. On their trolley rides, high on the sides of smoke-blackened buildings, he sees faded signs in lettering he can't read but knows is old. That the signs have accidentally survived but mean nothing fills him with dread and wonder, and he asks if the companies are still there, *Isidor Ash, Iron-Monger.* Those three and four-digit telephone numbers, do they still work, who do you get if you call, an imprisoned voice? Where do they all go?

He thinks of Hans von Kaltenborn and Gabriel Heatter and all the singers as being inside the radio. He presses his forehead against the back of the radio, inhaling the hot electric thrill of music from faraway cities, watching for miniature Jack Bennys and Edgar Bergens. 'Be very quiet, and quick, they'll run if they see you,' his mother says. In 1945, his father calls all the men on the street over to study the first sketches of the 1946 Ford, with headlights in the fenders and no running boards. When the war is finally over he promises to junk their '38 Packard for one of these streamlined babies.

Nineteen-forty-five means the children gather at the top of the dead-end street to intercept their fathers as they turn in, to be swept to their driveways like young footmen standing on the running boards and clinging to the mirrors and spotlights. The loudest kids live across the street. They're the three sons of the football coach at Duquesne. In the winter, he sleds with his father, held tight in his lap while two of the coach's sons stand on a toboggan and pass them, arguing about the war. We'll win because the Russians are on our side and Russians are eight feet tall.

In the winter, his mother piles up old papers and boards around the edge of their five-by-five porch off the kitchen and floods it in order to teach him ice-skating. She ties a pillow around him and lets him walk around the edges of the porch. His feet and ankles are undefined, like pillows. Coming down hard on an ankle, a hip, an arm, can crack a bone. But his father is Canadian and his parents met there and they skated and skied together before he was born. Knowing how to skate makes him a better son. It is important to his father and to his doctor for him to pass for normal as soon as possible.

They live on a crowded street at the edge of a heavily wooded valley that surrounds a tributary of the Allegheny River. In the winter, his father and the football coach ski down a path they have cleared to the rocks and boulders that mark the stream-bed. He's older than the coach, but a better skier and skater. 'What a beautiful animal your father is,' his mother says, watching him from the porch. On clear winter days, a rarity in Pittsburgh in those years, he can see through the blackened branches to the top of the Gulf Building and red lights on Mt. Washington. Willi transplants all his mother's night-time readings of Robin Hood into those woods. It is Sherwood Forest. Pittsburgh is Nottingham. The deer and bear and Merry Men are all out there, somewhere.

In the spring, when the ice is a morning's whitened blister over the concrete, the porch becomes his mother's studio. The buds have not yet opened, yet she arranges her paints and papers on the card table and carries out a chair to do her watercolours. She puts Mozart records on to play and keeps the kitchen door open so she can hear.

She brought her paints and bundles of drawings from Europe. Everything else is lost. Her brushes burst with colours that never drip. It reminds the boy of Disney cartoons, when a full paintbrush washes over the screen, creating the world as it touches down. That's how her paintings grow. Her colours seem especially intense, and have German names which never have satisfactory equivalents in English. He doesn't know they're enemy words; he thinks of them as irreplaceable tablets of pure colour. He laughs at *dunkelblau*, a funny word that becomes a code between them. Sometimes a fat man is Herr Dunkelblau. The last volumes of *My Book House* where the stories require too much explaining, are deep blue, dunkelblau. Other times she lies in bed behind closed window shades, holding her head with a dunkelblau. The opposite of dark, *dunkel*, he knows is *hell*, light.

'Watercolour must come down like rain,' she says. 'It should come quick like a shower and make everything shine, like rain. But it should not touch everything, not like oils.' Oils sound old and dutiful, like the museum.

'A paintstorm,' he says.

She sets him up with his paper and brushes and Woolworth's paints though he sometimes sneaks a swipe of her colours, thick and gripping as mud on his brush. Every few minutes she has to blow soot off her paper. When her German paints are gone, she'll quit painting.

She's a woman of Old World habits. Mondays and Fridays she does the wash. Because of the soot she has to take down all the white curtains, beat the rugs and bedspreads, take off the slipcovers and scrub the white shirts whose collars come back each day so black they look dipped in ink. Tuesdays are dyeing days, mixing the boxes of Rit that line the window ledge over the washtubs, to bring lime green to a Pittsburgh winter, or dunkelblau to a hot summer. Thursdays she makes the soap. Antiseptic odours fill the house, making his eyes run. Orange cakes of fresh soap are cut into shapes of states and countries. The shirts and sheets sink into the hot tub where she adds broken cakes of soap, and he adds the drops of blue-ing, and loses himself in the smoky trail of its dispersion. Such excitement for a child, catching the world in one of its paradoxes: adding stains to make clothes whiter. He can watch it spread forever, like watching cigarette smoke rise from his mother's ashtray or from the stubs his father burns down to nothingness, the smoke going straight up then suddenly hitting an invisible barrier and spreading out. On cleaning days, he's allowed to play in the coal bin, reading the old marks and dates of deliveries from before he was born, and throw his clothes in at the last minute, standing against the cold enamel of the washing tub as the islands of his shirt and pants and underwear resist, then drown.

Wednesdays she does the shopping, which means an afternoon of baking breads and an evening of stirring the bright orange colour tabs into the margarine. It's another low-grade art experience, like the blueing, with the added pleasure of being able to eat some of the results, melted over a bowl of Puffed Rice.

In the late summer of 1945, the war in Europe is over and the spirit on the radio is always upbeat. The arrival of troop ships is announced and train schedules from New York or Los Angeles tell Pittsburghers where to meet their boys. His mother listens for news of Europe, but there's never enough. Nineteen-forty-five is a year to gladden everyone but her. 'Just because you're German and you lost?' he asks her once, remembering the taunt of the coach's sons, and she runs from the room. He asks her who the best singer is – Bing Crosby, she says – and the funniest person – Bob Hope, she guesses, though they both prefer Jack Benny – and the prettiest woman – she couldn't say, ladies don't know who's pretty that way, but maybe he could ask his father – so, okay, the handsomest man – Van Johnson, they say – but the men she thinks are handsomer aren't around any more.

Nineteen-forty-five is the happiest year in his father's life and in the lives of the men on their street, whose jobs will all be getting bigger. There'll be houses to buy and new businesses to open and of course new cars, especially new cars. They're all thinking of leaving Pittsburgh. The Depression mentality is over, they've won the war, they're Number One in the world. But everything about 1945 makes his mother sadder, especially everyone's happiness. She shows him pictures of old men and women and children in striped pyjamas. 'So now we know that men are hideous beasts,' she says. 'What kind of world is this?' Nineteen-forty-five is the saddest year in existence. His father says it's like a sickness, her questions. You're crazy, he says. We'll all be rich if she'll just shut up and give him a chance.

She's busier than ever on the afternoons when the housework and shopping are done, painting the full, dark green summer of August, 1945. The atom bomb ends the war with Japan. He watches the woods and asks her if that isn't a bit of smoke rising through the trees, coming from the bottom of the woods, along the riverbank.

His father's winter ski-run offers a sightline through the woods if he goes between their house and Hutchisons' and stretches out on his stomach and peers down it as far as he can. He sees nothing at first, just the collapse of the vanishing point into a thicket of trees, but then he sees something: men, and maybe a horse. Horses in the woods! The woods are uninhabited, vast and practically virgin timber. When he shouts 'Men!' and 'Horses!' his mother says, 'Oh, God!' and puts her brush in a glass of clean water.

They go out the front of the house, to the top of the street. They walk down a block, turn and come to another dead-end street much like theirs, but poorer. The houses are low and wooden, more like sheds or garages. Their house is brick. Dogs and chickens run over the yards. Where the street abuts on a different part of the woods, a rutted path eases down into the dark. From there, they can see what the forest has given birth to: many men and some children, and two horses pulling a wagon.

'Gypsies!' she whispers.

Already the women on the street are chasing down their dogs and loose chickens. They stand at the top of the trail and shout at the wagoneers in words he can't understand. 'It's Polish,' his mother says. 'They're warning them not to come too close.' Children come out of the houses, carrying utensils and beating them with spoons.

'Stay close,' she says.

They wait for the wagon to mount the hill. The wagon is fat, ready to split, decked out in bells and leather straps with metal pots hanging from the corners. The men wear black hats with silver disks around the brims. There are no women. There are boys with long curly hair under their hats and men with open shirts and blackened arms beating spoons against the pots making a kind of chant. Street dogs are howling. The gypsies stop the noise just in front of the line of Polish women, and the boys lower the cart's back gate to expose a stone wheel operated by an old, white-haired man. The man wears an earring, something the boy has never seen, and it frightens him.

She wants him to watch. She holds him up, as she does in front of the paintings at the Library. And then she walks the length of the wagon with him, peering inside. 'You should see and not be frightened,' she says. The gypsies don't seem to care. The gypsy children follow them, laughing, and pull at his mother's skirt.

'Stop it!' she commands. 'You're very ill-behaved.'

They pull again.

'Brats! *Bengeln!*'

They giggle louder. *'Unverschämt!'*

When she speaks harshly like that, she's usually very angry and usually the person she's angry with, his father, does not understand. Bad behaviour is the only thing that gets her angry. Other things make her sad. Finally one of the men inside the wagon barks out a command and the children back off.

'Come to my street when you finish,' she says, pointing over the row of low, unpainted houses. 'I have some things.' The Polish women are now lined up with knives and scissors and some large cooking pots.

In one of the dark blue *Book Houses* there's a picture of a gypsy man holding a white horse in the moonlight, calling under a girl's window. For Willi, gypsies are a people out of the dream world of pictures and legends, and this is the first time he's seen something from his books come alive. In his light green world of *Book House* the pictures are all of talking animals. Later on they become magicians in tall caps decorated with stars and moons, then knights on horseback, Crusaders, and explorers. He's not given up the notion that their woods contain Robin Hood and his men, and now that it's given birth to gypsies, he takes heart again.

They hurry back to their house and his mother empties all the kitchen drawers and takes out the pots and pans and cake dishes, everything metal that is scratched or dented or has grown dull. She bundles them in a sheet and lays them on the front lawn. Then she grabs her drawing pad and some pencils and starts sketching from the front of the house. It's the first time she's sketched the street and not the woods. The beauty, she says, is all in the back.

In the front are houses just like theirs, and an open lot across the street where the larger boys play football and fathers play catch with their sons. He can't play – any shock can still shatter his bones. The opposite side of the street is much higher than theirs, even the empty lot is higher than the roof of their house. He can stand on the grass and see over his house and over the woods all the way to the Gulf Building. In other summers the sons of the football coach batted tennis balls and scuffed-up golf balls into high arcs over his house and the Hutchisons' into the trees and valley beyond.

Before the gypsies turn the corner, with the distant banging of the pots and clanging of the bells, and then the sharp cracking of the horsewhip, his mother has sketched in the roof lines, the trees, and the open lot. She's gotten the big tricycles in the driveways and one parked car.

'Gypsies! Lock your houses, take in your children, mind your dogs!' women on the street yell out, but soon enough they stand in their driveways clutching their knives and cooking pots. His mother pulls the covering sheet off her pile of metal utensils and tells a man everything needs polishing and sharpening and smoothing out, and she doesn't care how long it takes. By the time they're finished, she's gotten their picture, every detail in place with her pencils and charcoal: the horses, the children in their hats chasing dogs, all the clutter the wagon contains. She keeps sharpening her pencils against a block of sandpaper. She ignores the children who watch over her shoulder. Normally she stops anything she's drawing in order to demonstrate. When they leave, her arms are shaking, her hair is sticking to her forehead.

Later, when she sprays fixative, she says she hasn't worked so hard since her days at art school. She adds the drawing to her oldest sketches, those of German cathedral doors and Egyptian pottery and Nefertiti's head from the Berlin Museum, and country scenes of cows and horses and farmers bundling hay.

'A drawing should show everything,' she says, and that's what she likes about the gypsies; they are art, frightening and fascinating, their wagons are beautiful because they totally express the lives they lead.

'The war was fought over people like them,' she says. 'And people like us.'

But the gypsies don't go away. Smoke from their encampment

drifts up from the riverside, settles in a blue haze with the rest of Pittsburgh's smog. Through the early fall they're a familiar sight on the streets, and gradually the girls and women appear too, dressed in bandanas and wide colourful skirts. They come to the front doors, bold as you please, the neighbours say, offering to do housework and tell fortunes, selling eggs and strange-smelling flowers so strong they can drug you in the night. His mother draws the line at letting gypsies in the house. She doubts the wide skirts are purely a fashion statement.

As the leaves turn and drop they can see through to the encampment. There are four wagons and several cooking fires. His mother sketches it all, the ghostly outlines of the wagons through the tracery of branches, the horses, the pen for animals rumoured but unseen – bears, panthers, half-tamed wolves. It's a curious relationship she has with gypsies, to admire but not to trust, to adore as subjects while wishing they'd leave. The boy wants them gone. They excite his mother and make her strange. The gypsies are closer than he'd thought possible. He can hear them at night.

The assault begins with the coach's sons. They throw crushed limestones from the open lot across the street. They bat stones and golf balls, they use slingshots and their well-trained arms. They sneak down the slope and throw from the Nadeaus' side of the street, even from the corridor between their house and the Hutchisons', until his mother chases them off. From the sharp whinny of the horses, the barking and the occasional echo of stones on wood or metal, he knows the stones are striking home.

In early November the gypsies leave. 'West Virginia,' people say, a proper place for gypsies. Winter comes and the snows. His father and the coach are back on their ski run and the boy is strong enough to skate across the flooded porch. His father's plans are to leave Sears and go south, now that the country is back to normal. No more Carnegie Library, no more streetcar numbers to memorize and maybe he'll never get a card for the adult reading room. When his father mentions the word 'south' his mother shudders and leaves the room.

Being European, she doesn't believe in baby-sitters. She doesn't leave him until he is strong enough to walk on his own and be careful with appliances. On New Year's Eve they're invited to a party next door at Hutch and Marge's, friends of his father, a gregarious man. It's a cold, snowless night and he's allowed to sleep in the living room on the sofa with the radio on to see if he can stay awake for 1946. His mother promises she'll come over and wake him.

The Christmas tree is up, the electric train circles the wrinkled sheet city of snowy hills. When he wakes up with only the tree lights on, the radio is humming but not playing music and he thinks he must have slept through everything. Nineteen-forty-five is the first year of his consciousness, the year of his true birth, and now it is over. It has died, and he is born. The worst year in history, his mother says. The best, his father counters. He gets up and looks next door to Hutch and Marge's where a light is on and it looks close enough to run to, barefoot in his pyjamas.

The door is open and the vestibule is jammed with fur coats. The air inside is hot and thick with smoke and forced, loud laughter. His father and the coach are the oldest men in the room, and the loudest and happiest. Theirs is a young street of mainly childless couples ready now to start their families. The women are getting pregnant, there's a sharp bite of sexuality in the air, lives are going places but still on hold, the country is going places, big places, but hasn't quite gotten over its wartime gloom and pinchpenny habits. Those are the attitudes he hears and takes as truth. He sides with his father in the arguments because his father's a great one for looking ahead, on the bright side, to the future. The aluminum Train of Tomorrow is barrelling down the tracks, taking them all to a chrome-plated, streamlined, lightweight future and cities like Pittsburgh with their dirty bricks and labour problems are in the way of progress. If you're in the way, better clear out. A damned shame some people just can't get in the spirit.

'And you think the south is progress?' his mother demands.

His father is singing, with his back to the fireplace. Not French songs, the way they usually ask him to at parties, but Bing Crosby songs. Around the mirror over the mantel, Hutch and Marge have pasted all their Christmas cards. Their tree is bigger than the Nadeaus', and the lights blink and some other candles bubble. Everyone is outlined in blue and red and faint ghostly yellow. All the women except his mother are blondes, with big round coral earrings and bright lipstick that stains their cigarettes. Some still wear little hats with their veils half pulled down.

He stands in the hallway, leaning against a fur coat, peering around the edge. They're singing the New Year's Song his mother taught him, and they're blowing on paper trumpets and strapping on little cone-shaped hats. His mother stands at the far end of the living room, by the kitchen door where the light is strongest. *I don't feel like celebrating,* she declared earlier and his father had left on his own, shouting, *You can't ruin it for me,* but she went anyway, a few minutes later. He peels off his pyjamas and wraps himself in her fur coat. No one notices him. Her head is down and her hands hold the sides of her face, pressing down her veil. She seems to be rocking back and forth. Someone has set a lime-green party hat on top of her black pillbox with the single pheasant feather.

They're counting backwards. When the numbers get smaller, the noise increases and he's shouting with everyone, trailing the heavy coat, 'It's 1946! It's 1946!' running naked into the living room like the Baby New Year with the sash. A few women hug him and squeeze him tight in their unsteadiness. His father looks around to see how he's gotten there – he has Marge and another woman on his arms – and all the men are going around collecting kisses.

'For God's sake, Liesl –' his father calls and she drops to her knees with her arms open as he pushes his way to her through a jitterbugging dance floor. It seems to take hours. She rolls up her veil to touch her eyes with a paper napkin.

Her fur coat falls from his shoulders as she lifts him. He rubs his cheek against the rough and the fine mesh of her veil, feels her cool satin dress against his naked body, and they dance. It seems the whirling will go on forever, even as the music dies out, then the laughter, and he and his mother dance their way out the door, shivering, across the icy grass to home.

Snake in Flight over Pittsburgh

TWO YOUNG MEN – boys, really – are playing chess in a living room in Pittsburgh in the late summer of 1960. Their shoes are polished, they wear flannel pants with white suspenders, formal shirts with pearl studs, maroon bowties and cummerbunds. Their jackets are on the sofa. They are eighteen, home from their first year of college. Terry has gone from high school honours to Princeton honours. Alex has struggled through the year at Oberlin. Nothing serious; just a confirmation that absolutes do exist in the world, and Terry, who plays better chess and who'd gotten better grades and who goes to a more competitive school is by all accounts smarter than Alex.

Before a spurt of growth that cleared his skin and lifted him to well over six feet, Terry had been a pimply, bulb-headed boy with an air of incipient officiousness. Alex, who had been much taller, hasn't grown since: he's average, but beginning to fade. Already his hair-parting is suspiciously wide, and a bay had opened between his temple and forehead to receive it. He can still easily hide a tiny tonsure that marks the confluence of the combed latitudes over the vault of his skull and the thick, brushed longitudes down the back. Soon, he'll look like Adlai Stevenson. Europe, he calls his widening forehead, mowing down the jungles behind. He is particularly aware of his bald spot when Francesca stands behind him as he crouches over the chess board, not that she's likely to, today.

Ironically, they had met in an eighth-grade moment of shared equality. In high school, Terry had gotten only two A's. One was in English, the other in German. Alex had also managed just two A's, in the same two courses. In their intensely competitive school, however, every letter grade was sliced three ways – plus, plain and minus – and every other grade of Terry's had been A+. Most of Alex's had been A- (a particularly apt, almost evocative judgement, he's come to feel) when not B+ (the cruelest mark of all), or even a solid B. He considers himself at best an A- person in a B- world. Terry is something else, entirely.

Alex is in love with the whole concept of Terry Franklin's family: his being, his house, his parents, his relatives, his younger brothers and especially, his twin sister. They favour simple things, quality goods bought in cash, when not home-made. Terry's chess set is home-made, something fashioned in a Scoutish summer out of clothespins. What a marvellous thing it is, to Alex's mind, not to lose things, to be living in the only house you've ever known, to have parents at home, and to fashion bishops, rooks and knights from simple tacks, nails and various screws. The king wears an eye-hook. Terry has ridden that modest set to the big leagues of amateur chess in Western Pennsylvania – a 2200 ranking from the USCF. Alex thinks of that chess set as somehow the proof of true talent, the phenom's arrival with patched shoes and a slab of leather who shames the American Legion boys in their flannel suits with twenty-dollar Spaldings and bevelled cleats.

There are rumours of lineage, of a remote ancestor from Philadelphia, perhaps not quite legitimate. In the 19th century a certain Benj Franklin had crossed the Alleghenies and established the family on vast tracts south of the present city. His mother's family, mountaineers and moonshiners, according to more legend, had been in the hills since the Revolution. Both sides have been there ever since.

Terry's parents, Alex is convinced, lie at the heart of their son's achievement, which is another way of saying *his* parents are to blame for his relative mediocrity. Dr Franklin, a research chemist at Westinghouse, is older than most fathers. He'd established himself in the world before getting married. Terry does not remember him other than grey and bald, yet he has never bested his father in any competition. Dr Franklin still drives the lane against Terry's guarding, still sinks his free-throws twenty in a row, still sculls on weekends as he had forty years earlier at MIT. He heads a nature group, publishes a bird-watchers' letter, advises the Scouts, and chairs the local Republican Committee. He's a senior in the United Presbyterian Church, and still, he reads. Greek and Latin. The classic novels, the latest biographies, histories. The house is full of books, none of them in paperback.

Of course, Alex exempts Dr Franklin from *too* much knowledge, or *too* proper an attitude. Alex has gone on a demonstration against segregated housing in Cleveland, and he's attended a couple of meetings of a local SNCC chapter. He's heard enough around the Franklin table over the years to know what the family believes: people prefer to live and to travel with their own kind, though Alex's activism is tolerated, even respected, in an amused sort of way. Actually, he'd been grandstanding just a bit. He hadn't gone on the Greyhound trip to Memphis and Nashville. And he had left the picket line in Cleveland before the police broke it up.

He'd been trying to impress Francesca. She'd been eating at home that night, a rare event, and not with her boyfriend. Alex looked on each night he was at the Franklins' – which was most nights – as his last chance to save her. His last chance at personal happiness. Any day now, his future would open before him, and he would stumble into a profession or a set of attitudes, something as simple for others but impossible for him as a distinctive haircut or clothing style or political attitude that would reflect or perhaps define the man he sensed within him.

Alex has often wondered what, exactly, accounts for their friendship. He is grateful for it – without it, he might have died – but he never quite understood it. He and Terry have nothing in common. If he has sympathies, they are with the arts, with chaos, destruction. If he has ruling passions, they are bitterness and resentment and monstrous self-pity.

On the day he met Terry, all the eighth-graders had written personal essays entitled 'My Typical Day'. His had been slightly lurid – he was a natural exaggerator – and the teacher had gone out of her way to praise it. Alex and his family were new to Pittsburgh, the latest stop in their gypsy existence. He'd exaggerated that as well. His parents had started a furniture store in a squalid satellite town, one of those cinders in space that never quite became a suburb, and they were at it eighteen hours a day, freeing Alex for sleeping and rising, meals and entertainment, entirely on his own. He was an only child who went to movies alone on week-nights, stayed up late for Jack Paar, and exercised greasy options for dinner each night, mindless of milk and vegetables.

He sees now what Terry was driving at. How vulnerable he is to the charms Terry can offer. They live in a world of mutual envy, a Mexican stand-off of incredulity.

Alex resents anything that separates himself from communion with the Franklins. He resents being shorter and slower and less co-ordinated, less intelligent and clean-featured, less noble and religious, less hard-working and clearly committed, less universally admired, less socketed in the community. He resents the smells of his parents' apartment, the stale, bluish air, and having parents – nobodies from nowhere – who smoke and leave their bottles around the house, who wouldn't mind if he smoked and drank, and give him no credit for choosing not to, who've failed so miserably in so many undertakings.

The Franklins go back at least five generations in Pittsburgh, and none of them, apparently, has known a Pittsburgh life of mill-work, squalor, black-lung, or Catholicism. Hardly any of the aunts and uncles and sturdy, reliable cousins that Alex has come to know by the dozens in the past five years, smoke, drink, or even swear.

Alex has suffered through a bad freshman year at Oberlin. The only girls he's dated have been civil rights activists who encourage his liberalism – given his wretched class origins he's something of an aberration – but who duck into Cleveland for weekends to test their 'existential commitment' with black men in the ghetto. He's awash in self-pity, fearing himself short-changed in the manhood department. Terry suggests they're just the wrong girls for him.

'You know who's right for you, don't you? Francesca? She's been after me for years about you.'

Terry found a girl at Vassar who's visited him twice this summer in Pittsburgh, when the tennis tour makes it convenient. She's on the Vassar freshman team, nationally ranked, a Davis Cup prospect.

She can give Terry more than a good game. Terry won their club's junior championship; he's not accustomed to losing anything, and he doesn't make an especially appealing spectacle of himself, whaling away from the baseline against Susan Stanbury's powerful returns. Alex, with club privileges, has standing invitations to swim or play. He has never held a racquet. His parents have never belonged to anything that requires a vote.

She's on tour today, and can't be here for the wedding. It may cause a break-up, though Terry's too well-mannered to deliver ultimatums. Susan is a small blond girl with chopped-off hair and a pug nose. She favours pearls, but smells of chlorine. Alex doesn't credit her with much sexuality or any charm – her whole conversation consists of tennis terms and tour dates and pointers for Terry's game – though at least she'd not sneak off to ghetto hotels to test her commitment. Her father is an investment banker in New York. Terry visited her there in the winter and has been taken to dinner at the Princeton Club. It is hard for Alex even to imagine his Pittsburgh friend, accomplished as he is, a boy of undoubted genius who'd been too busy to date in high school, whose family ties are so strong he's never eaten in a restaurant, never spent money at a movie or at a sporting contest, never been a fan – only a participant – actually *finding* a girl and apparently knowing what to do with her and how to keep it going over a Pittsburgh summer, which can blight nearly anything.

He resents the way the Franklins embrace the girl, how Francesca takes her downtown on the assumption that a couple of dates with her brother and a visit will result in a marriage and move to Pittsburgh. 'We'll be sisters!' she cried, a stomach-turning proposal, thinks Alex. She can say goodbye to Sak's Fifth Avenue and Lord & Taylor and say hello to Kaufman's and Joseph Horne's. Pittsburgh at least had a Gimbel's which can take her credit card.

'How marvellous you're a Presbyterian, too!' Mrs Franklin had observed. 'I didn't think there *were* any in New York City.'

Alex has loved Francesca since the day in the eighth grade, after his first dinner at their house. He'd been impressed and a little frightened by the elaborate 'Grace' participated in by all. They held hands under the table. He was seated between the twins and hadn't known Terry was, as it were, duplicated (they looked nothing alike, nor were their accomplishments in any way similar). Francesca had missed a year due to a childhood illness; she was the tallest and prettiest seventh-grader in the school.

He was sure she'd forget him, but the next day at school she called out, 'Hi, Alex,' and stood by his locker as he loaded books and forgot what he needed, forgot where he was going. She walked with him down the corridor, carrying her books in a young girl's swaying manner, against an emerging bosom. She cocked her head to hear him better though he had nothing to say and they were the same height anyway. People had seen them together, that's what mattered, and they didn't look, he felt, implausible.

That had been his moment. He knew five years ago she was going to be beautiful (but never *this* beautiful, so much beauty he couldn't look on her), and more: kind, intelligent without arrogance.

'She asked about you,' Terry would say. 'Always asks me, when's Alex going to ask me out?'

'Oh, sure,' he'd say, usually over chess.

'She says she thinks about you all the time.'

'Oh, for Christ's sake, Terry. What makes you think I care what she thinks?'

'Think how convenient it would be,' he'd say, back in the ninth and tenth grades. 'There's her room, there's an extra bed up here ... in the middle of the night, who would know?'

'Just cut it out, okay?'

'Is that a blush I see?'

She still wasn't taken, back then. She'd have a date or two but nothing serious. Francesca, genetically incapable of imperfection, achieved a quality altogether different from Terry's. She has height, fair hair, and a model's high-planed features. She has Terry's intelligence but not his ambition. She has warmth and humour, a suppressed laughter that Alex can feel just by looking at her, as though together (he fantasizes) they are sharing a joke at the world. She has open sympathies with liberal causes.

Just last month after dinner, she'd come downstairs, dressed to go out with her boyfriend, the one she'd gotten serious about while Alex was away at Oberlin. The boyfriend was more than that; they all called him, facetiously, he hoped, her fiancé. He was a college senior, a threat Alex had to take seriously. A Harvard senior, with many attributes that come easily to Harvard men, like a sportscar and easy manners and helpful contacts in the business world through his father, who was, like Susan Stanbury's father, an investment banker. As Francesca was coming downstairs, Terry met her halfway up and gave her breast a noticeable jiggle and pinch, something that caused her to frown and push away.

Her father was at the base of the stairs. 'Problem, honey?'

'Just him.'

'Terry? You have something to say to your sister?'

Francesca pulled a little at her sweater.

'I told my sister she was looking very nice for her young man,' Terry replied. 'She must have misunderstood. I'll have to learn to speak more clearly.'

'I think so, too,' said Dr Franklin. 'What do you think, Alex?'

He was afraid at that moment of saying too much, of emptying all the grief in his heart and reducing the nature of his relationship with that marvellous family to a sham. In a word or two he might have acknowledged all that Terry suspected of his motives and held implicitly over him. He merely shrugged and muttered, 'Okay, I guess.'

'That's all, Alex? Only okay?' She sounded hurt. Then came that suppressed little laugh as she pointed a finger at Terry. ' "If you like that sort of thing," ' she said in a mocking voice, 'is that it? Just an ugly sister who gets in the way and doesn't play chess and doesn't like some of the other games her brother plays – okay for someone like that, is that it?'

And by then she was at the base of the stairs with her father and Alex. Terry had gone up to his lab. 'Alex is right, daddy.' She picked up on a dinner conversation. She was folding a pastel scarf to tie over her hair, a sign that she and her Harvard boy were going driving. 'I'd vote for Kennedy, too, if I were old enough.'

'Oh, heaven forbid!' her father gasped with a theatrical groan. 'Sharper than a serpent's tooth.'

She stands on the porch waiting for her date. Alex is suddenly alone downstairs. He could go out to the porch and stand with her – she'd like that, it would even appear a little gallant, plausible, to neighbours. He yearns to join her, a last chance to stop the future, even for the sweet pain of turning her over to her Harvard Buzz. He could do it, he thinks, even at this late hour, say the things and make them count. Reveal his secret identity. Show her that it had been *his* love, all these years, not her father, not the church, not the ghastly Buzz, that maintained her, kept her safe, kept her whole. Kept her brother from her. *He* was the engine that drove the Franklin family, the heat, the light. He could make her know it, now. But he hates the way it would look. He's not a bird-dog.

'Alex,' Dr Franklin turns midway up the stairs. 'I don't think your father got as good a deal as he hoped. You might ask him about it.' Then he's gone, up to his study to work on his Latin, to read his Bible, and eventually to join his wife in sleep. Terry is working. Francesca waits. The needle Dr Franklin has just inserted is more painful to him than the thought of Buzz blaring the horn of his Belvedere just outside.

Dr Franklin, in his methodical way, has discovered that Alex's father cheated him badly. What he perhaps doesn't know is that the cheating is deliberate. When his parents started their store, his role had been to enlist his friends' support. 'See that all your rich friends get the word,' his father said. 'Tell them they'll get the deal of a lifetime.' The Franklins had come around late, but they'd finally come, cash in hand, for three bedrooms' worth. A few weeks after the sale he'd heard his mother shouting, 'How *could* you? That's despicable!'

His father was silent, as usual.

'*Borax!*' she cried.

'So? I'm Borax. I know what I am. You see jerks, you take them for a ride. You make your breaks in this world. You don't mind spending it, so don't complain about how you get it. You think maybe this jerk'll give us a break on a Westinghouse refrigerator? Well, I got news for you. It don't work that way. Nobody gets a break.'

He determined that night, listening to them fight, that he would hate his father and the business he was in and the world that had created him, and he would pray for its failure and destruction, in the name of the Franklins and all the others he'd been forced to defraud. Worse than anything, it was the bed that Francesca slept on, and the dresser she stored her sweaters in, the nightstand and lamp she read by, the desk she did her work on, that they had sold the Franklins.

Today might be the saddest day of Alex's life. Upstairs, Francesca is preparing herself for sacrifice. She's graduated from high school and turned down her scholarship to Bryn Mawr in order to marry Buzz Howarth, her Harvard boy. His father is buying them a 'cottage' – his word – in Cambridge. Francesca will keep house a year, start a family – she's anxious for that, according to Terry – then maybe when Rod (his real name, a word so pulsatingly ugly, so grotesquely appropriate, that Alex can barely utter it) starts the B-School, she'll go to B.U. or Tufts, at night. She's eighteen. She'll never see college, never date, never hear from other men anything of her exquisiteness.

She's been seen and claimed by a college man whose family doesn't cheat on principle and whose aunt is a friend of the Franklins through the Church, the Republicans and the Women's Club. That's how they'd met. The Harvard nephew visits his aunt, the aunt takes him on her Club rounds one day, Francesca accompanies her mother to deliver some cookies to the same charity, and like a drunk swerving over the centre-stripe, there'd been a horrible, utterly unnecessary collision, resulting in marriage.

The relatives have gathered. The neighbourhood girls, the bridesmaids, have been in and out all day, brushing past the two college boys in fancy clothes playing chess but not really moving pieces.

Alex remembers his last time with her, the only chance conferred by the gods to thwart her fate. Three weeks before, she'd spoken to him on a Saturday morning, after breakfast. He'd slept over that night and been poking around the silent kitchen for cereal. He'd not known about a wedding, no one had mentioned it. Buzz wasn't a fiancé yet. There still was time to disallow this infatuation with a tall good-looking guy who'd decided to spend his summer in Pittsburgh working at the Mellon Bank instead of New York in securities. Still time to stand in the middle of the track and raise his hand against the 20th Century Limited, stopping it inches from her trussed-up body.

'Alex? Would you do me a big favour?'

She was dressed in a Harvard sweatshirt many sizes too large, in blue jeans, with her hair tied back in a pony-tail. 'I've got a doctor's appointment downtown.' She held out the keys to their family car. She'd never learned to drive. All the other Franklins could have been issued licences in the first grade.

He knew their family doctor, but this one was different. She didn't seem concerned, but what kind of illness requires a Saturday appointment on Diamond Street? He could never stare directly at her as he wanted to, but he had the impression of unusual pallor, a bit of fatigue about the eyes. She'd come in past midnight the night before. Up on the third floor, Alex had heard it. Terry had timed it, from the arrival of the car to the opening of the door. Fifty-seven minutes, a record, he said. 'How time flies when you're having fun.'

He parked on the street, not difficult on a Saturday morning, and waited for her in the car. It was like a date. It was almost like a marriage. She trusted him with something, his discretion, though he sensed it was more. He feared she was in pain, even as he sat there, helpless and ignorant. Or that she was at this moment undressing before a man who would slide a stethoscope between her breasts. He thought of the word 'disrobe' and shivered.

She was back in twenty minutes, surprised, it seemed, that he'd even waited. 'I could have taken the streetcar back.' She seemed almost angry.

'I wanted to.'

'Why?'

The words *I love you* almost came out. They were as close to his lips as they'd ever been. 'What else am I going to be doing? I may as well haul you around.'

'How very gallant we are this morning. All I had to do was get my thing fixed.'

'What thing?'

'So I could use it later,' she laughed. 'That's between us. Now home, please, Alex.'

When they were on the Duquesne Bridge she said, out of the silence that he'd been wanting to break, 'I've always wondered about something – will you give me an honest answer?' It was a warm day, but his hands turned icy.

'About what?'

'You. Promise you won't get angry.'

'You couldn't get me angry.'

'Okay, then. What I've always wanted to know is, how can you *stand* to come over to our house, week after week? Are you a masochist or something? I really want to know.'

He'd been preparing himself to confess his love, his parents' crimes, his collusion. But this, the foundation of his very existence? 'I like your place.'

'*Really?*'

'I want a family just like yours. I *want* to be like your father –'

'Really?'

'A wife, I mean, a marriage, like –'

'You want a wife like my mother? Honestly?'

'Well –'

'Tell me.'

They were just entering the Ft Pitt Tunnels. It is one of the scenes he will carry for life, every stone-face etched, the heaped red lights of a dozen cars dribbling before him into the dark. He can hear his voice even now, an adolescent delivering Cyrano, all the worse because they are true, precisely his feelings.

'I want a wife, just like you.'

Let me die, he thought. Let an avalanche come down. '*You're* why I come. It's only to see you. It's always just to see you.' And then they were in the tunnel, one of those perfectly innocent natural symbols that Pittsburgh especially provides. He needed full control, both hands on the wheel of an unfamiliar station wagon, but he knew it was a moment for reaching out. If they could only stop, he would be met half-way.

Say something, he prayed. They were out of the tunnel. The great truth had been uttered, the burden lifted, and nothing had changed. The same dull yearning, the same wish that he could cut out his tongue.

'I always wondered why you never called me Franny. You always call me Francesca.'

'That's how you were introduced to me. I didn't want to change anything.'

'But I was just a *kid!*'

'Never to me.'

'All those years, and you never even talked to me – I can't believe it. This isn't a joke, is it? What am I, scary?'

'To me you are.'

'What can I say – I'm flattered? I'm sorry? I just never even suspected. You're a good actor, Alex, you really are. Terry always said you didn't like me, and I believed him. He used to tell me the really disgusting names you called me.'

'I couldn't even mention your name.'

'He'd do the same thing to any boy who called me up. No one ever called me a second time. He said everyone figured you'd get around to asking me out, and that would be it. He said he'd work on you to, you know, close your eyes and take me out –'

'Stop it, please. I never, never –'

'That's okay.'

'No, I mean it, I –'

'I said it's all right. I'm not blaming you.' Her voice had changed. 'Terry wants to keep boys away from me and he wants someone he can –'

She broke off, and somewhere inside, his soul did a deep-dive.

'– someone to appreciate him, let's say, so he just found the perfect way of doing it. The worst thing that could possibly have happened was that he'd lose me to you. But you took care of that.'

'I was afraid to speak.'

'He chose you very well. Why not? – he's a very very clever boy. Why do you think *I'm* so friendly with that awful Susan? I want him to find somebody. *Anybody.* We've been together longer than we've been alive, and he won't let go. I suppose he told you about my illness?'

'He said you had some glandular thing.'

'And you believed him I suppose.'

'I didn't want to know.'

'Boy, Alex, if they handed out medals for curiosity. Why *didn't* you ask, if you cared so much? It's the first thing Rodney wanted to know.'

'I was afraid you might have suffered. I couldn't have taken that.'

'I *did* suffer, Alex. I suffered horribly. I had a breakdown. I was a mental case.'

She must have been exaggerating. 'I can't believe that.'

'I wouldn't expect you to. But for one whole year I didn't talk – did Terry tell you that? The doctors said I'd made up my mind that *I* was going to separate us, and the only way I could do it was to kill myself. But I was too young to do it, so I just stopped talking and then I stopped eating just so I wouldn't have to sit beside him in every class for twelve years. Franklin, F. and Franklin, T. like man and wife – I had dreams about school chairs with our names painted on them in blood and that's how the doctors discovered the problem. Does that make sense?'

'Now, yes.'

'Listen to me, Alex, I may be the one who *went* crazy, but he's the crazy one. He's incomplete. He needs another half. If he can't have me, he'll take you. Cut loose, really. I've already got someone, thank God, or else I'd help.'

She was staring out the window, mouth clenched tight, a look he'd seen before, her particular kind of anger. He knew all her looks, he knew so much about her, he thought. He could imagine a smaller version of her, looking out a window for a year in just that clenched silence.

She comes down the stairs early in the afternoon. In white, but the shoulders and bodice are sheathed in such fine muslin she looks, at first, half-nude. Terry whistles, Alex whirls in his seat, then turns back to the board. But Terry is advancing on her. 'Best man gets a kiss, right?' and she backs up a step. 'Terry, for heaven's sake, I have to make a phone call.'

'You can call, who's stopping you?' and Alex hears again, against the pounding of his own heart, 'My *make-up*, Terry, God! What's the matter with you today?' and when Alex finally stands and takes a step towards them, he sees his friend, hands on her shoulders, but slowly, playfully, tracing the patterns of white flowers while she stands, nearly his height, a step above him.

'Not bad. Nice work. Don't make 'em like this any more.'

'Ter-ry.'

'No, sir. They broke the sister mould when they made you. But don't tell me all *this* is real.' His hand is lower now, at the point where the solid satin joins the fine mesh, the point of greatest prominence, and his fingers make ever-smaller circles, looking for the sweetest place to land.

Alex takes his cue from the look of panic on her face. She pushes her brother, and Alex grabs his shoulder, and the effect is of a blind-side tackle. Terry has braced himself against her, but from Alex's touch he crumples, down one step and then down two more, falling heavily against the closet door like the villain in a Western fight, as though an enormously strong hero has picked him up and tossed him like a straw against the wall.

Terry says nothing; he's too well-bred. He smiles. A little horse-play, he might be saying, a payback for those hundreds of lost games of chess, Monopoly, Horse and anything else they've ever competed in. Leverage and surprise, and Terry has been humiliated for the first time in his life. Alex feels sure he'll hear about it in some other way.

'You must have been lifting weights, old friend,' he says, rubbing his neck. 'You pack a nasty wallop.' He's taken a small cut on his forehead. The plaster is dented in several places.

'Oh, come on, Terry. It's *her* day. She deserves respect.'

'She deserves,' says Terry, looking at his watch, then at his sister talking urgently on the phone, 'she deserves whatever she's going to get in approximately three hours and twenty-two minutes, depending on traffic. And don't you wish it was you.'

'Come on.'

'Don't you wish you *could*. Don't you wish –' then he drops it, with a smile. 'Well, wishing won't make it so. Or grow.'

'Terry, watch it.'

'Watch it? What's it going to do?'

'I'll fight you.'

Terry squares his shoulders but doesn't bother to put up his fists. 'Okay, I'm the host and you're the guest. Anything you want, any time you want it. That's the rule around here. At least, it always has been.'

Francesca whirls around, cheeks fiery, as though she'd been slapped.

'Terry! Alex! This is my wedding day – what do you think you're doing?' She shakes her brother. 'Get a hold of yourself. How long are you going to be like this?'

'How long?' he asks in a voice of sweet reasonableness. 'Gee, I wouldn't know. You ought to know by now.'

'You're disgusting. Talk to him, Alex. He's in one of his spells.' Very deliberately, she slaps him, a noise sharper than his crash into the closet door. 'Isn't best man good enough for you? Do you want me to ask Alex? Is that it?'

'I don't want to be your best man,' he says.

'Best man would in his case require a very complicated explanation,' says Terry.

'You shut up. I won't have you ruining the happiest day of my life.'

'And having him up front wouldn't?'

'Of course it wouldn't. I'd prefer it. I should have asked him from the beginning. Alex, will you please be our best man? Rod won't mind.'

'No,' he repeats.

'Honestly, he'd love it. Please, Alex, I can explain it.'

'Yep, good old Buzz thinks you're real Harvard material. "There's one that got away", that's what good old Buzz always says.'

'No,' he says again. He's staring into her face, just inches away.

'I've got an idea!' Terry interjects. 'Let *me* explain it to good old Buzz. Let me explain to him why I shouldn't be best man but my old buddy Alex should be. Would you trust me? Huh, sis?'

'*Sis,*' she repeats, a hiss. 'God, I hate you.'

'Only sometimes.'

Just then, a gaggle of her high school friends, all dressed in pink and beige formal dresses appear at the head of the stairs. 'Frannie, get up here! He's come! You can't let him see you!'

Her colour drains, she smiles, kisses her fingers and lays them on Alex's lips, then, reluctantly, on Terry's. 'May the better man win,' she whispers, then hikes her train for a quick ascent.

He's out in the backyard an hour later, by the flower bed under the crabapple tree – the fruits are starting to redden – where some of the uncles and cousins have tapped in the croquet wickets and are having a game. They are due at the church in about two hours, but there is time for family and guests, the people without formal duties. He is in his black satiny coat and grey vest, holding a dainty cup of Hawaiian punch. Terry has left for the church with his parents and Rod's family. Griff, one of Terry's younger uncles, is standing at the far corner of the yard, cupping a cigarette. He's the odd man in the family, reportedly a union man from West Virginia, married to Mrs Franklin's much younger sister. He's in his late twenties, wearing a Madras sports coat. Of all people, Buzz is standing with him, tapping his shoes with the end of a croquet mallet.

'Gotta get goin' soon,' Griff is saying. 'Whatya say, Alex?'

'Hey, Alex – great seeing you!' Buzz sweeps a paw in the general direction, and comes up with most of Alex's palm and wrist.

'Congratulations in advance.'

'Griff's giving me some pointers, here. Old married man, and all. Not every day a man gets married, you know.'

'You just missed a garden snake,' says Griff. 'Probably scared him when we started knocking croquet balls into the creepers.'

84

'Do you think Frannie's afraid of snakes, Alex?' Buzz asks. He stoops from the knees, not looking in his direction. 'You having known her so much longer, I mean.'

'You should ask her,' Alex says, and just then Buzz's hand darts out into the creepers and he snaps to attention with a two-foot garter snake clasped firmly behind the head. What kind of man catches a snake? He holds it out, like a man measuring a belt, and runs his other hand down its length, pinching it at the tail and flipping it over, letting the head hang down nearly to the grass. Actually, Francesca is terrified of snakes. Alex wonders if Buzz intends to shock her with one, a notion he endorses. He has a small, vanishing interest in the quick dissolution of their marriage.

Rod observes in a low voice to Griff and Alex, as he casually twirls the snake in slow arcs, attracting the stares and applause of some of the family, that he's always envied snakes. 'Just think, Griff, if you're a snake, every move you make in the grass could be an orgasm – ever think of that?'

He whirled the snake overhead, higher and faster, like a lariat, then let it go, an airborne eel against the summer sky. They chuckle their appreciation.

'Reckon we know what's on your mind,' says Uncle Griff.

'Boy!' he says, smiling modestly. 'If I don't see you again, Alex, it's been great. Frannie thinks the world of you.'

'And I of her,' he says.

Man and His World

IN THE SEASON of dust with the sun benign, a man of forty and a boy of twelve appeared at the Tourist Reception Centre, asking for rooms. Failing that, a house, with cook and servant.

The Centre was a modest concrete bunker with thirty rooms and a dining hall, and it was full. This was winter, the time for migrating Siberian songbirds and their Japanese pursuers. For the man and boy the situation was potentially desperate. Udirpur was a walled, medieval town baked on an igneous platter a thousand feet above the desert. To the east, no settlements for 200 kilometres. To the west lay twenty kilometres of burnt, rusted tanks and stripped, blood-stained Jeeps, a UN outpost manned by a bizarre assortment of ill-equipped troops, then barbed wire, mines, and fifteen kilometres of more trophy tanks and blood-stained Jeeps. In the winter, buses dropped off passengers twice a week, picked up freight, and returned to the capital.

The man – who gave his name as William Logan – really should have booked a room through the central authority. That way, he would have saved the trip, and who knows, maybe his life.

2. They had been on the road six days from New Delhi. Sleeping on buses, standing on trains, paying truckers. By day, the thin air required a sweater, though the hot sun could burn with its mere intention. From March, when summer returned, the town would disappear from tourist maps and the national consciousness. The national highway would become the world's longest clothesline and camel dung kiln.

Wealth was counted in camels. Camels outnumbered bicycles in the district. Camels pulled the wooden-wheeled carts and plodded around the water-screws, drawing up monsoon rains from the summer before. They yielded their carcasses more graciously than any animal in the world. The first sight of camels grazing in the bush had been a wonder to William Logan. Something half evolved to mammalhood, comic and terrifying in its brute immensity. It had confirmed him, for the moment, in the rightness of what he was doing.

In the desert near the Rat Temple, the government maintained a camel-breeding station. The sight of a hobbled cow being mounted by the garlanded bull, their bellows and the swelling of their reptilian necks, suggested to the Japanese naturalists on their guided tours an echo of the world's creation, a foretaste of its agony and death.

3. Before the invasion of the Aryans, Greeks, Persians and British, the desert people had their own cosmology. The Mother of the World had given birth to identical pairs of camels, tigers, gazelles, elephants and rats. She did not distinguish among her children. She did not have a particular aspect or appearance; whatever their size or ferocity, the children all resembled her, perfectly. The people of Udirpur are still known as rat-worshippers.

When she was nearly too old for child-bearing and the world was already full, she found herself pregnant again. And for the first time, she suffered pain, foreboding, fatigue. She bled, lay down frequently and grew thin. And from her womb came rumbles, lava, fire and flood. When she gave birth, only one cub emerged. His strangled, identical brother fell from the womb and was hastily buried under the great stone anvil in the middle of the desert.

It is said that one brother was evil, but which one? They had struggled in the womb but the secret was kept. The tribes of animals divided. Those giving allegiance to the survivor became his servants. Others retired to the oceans and to the air and to the underworld, growing fins or scales or feathers, or shrinking themselves to become insects. They all kept faith with the one who had died.

It is said that survivor, be he good or evil, is born with sin and with guilt and is condemned to loneliness. Nowhere on the earth will he find his brother or anything else like him. And with this birth, the Mother of the World died and the creative cycle came to an end.

4. Ten years earlier, from over the mountains a thousand kilometres to the north, a woman had arrived in Udirpur: the palest, whi-
test woman the people had ever seen. She'd been discovered outside
the Rat Temple by a lorry-driver who'd been praying to the God for
a successful trip. He had offered sweets and lain still while the
God's children swirled over his hands and feet, licking his still-
sweet fingers and lips.

Clearly the girl was a hippie – the only English word he knew –
one of a tribe he'd heard about but never seen. She carried a new-
born baby and nursed him like a village woman by the temple gates.
She wore a torn, faded sari, something the lorry-driver's own wife
or widowed mother would be ashamed to wear. But she wore it well
and seemed comfortable in it.

He spoke to her in his language, offering a ride to Udirpur, where
at least there were facilities for foreign women and for babies. To
his surprise, she answered in a language he knew. She gathered her
sleeping baby and the cotton sack that held her possessions and followed him to his truck, without question. This was the way she had
travelled and lived for the past three years. At some point in time
lost to her now, she had been a girl in a cold small town on the edge
of a forest, near a river frequented by whales. She had left that town
on a bus to work in the city in the year of a World's Fair. And after
that summer she'd not stopped her travelling, until it brought her
here.

The lorry-driver knew where to take her. In Udirpur, the city of
rats, the Raja had travelled the world. He spoke every language and
he welcomed whatever remnant of the world that managed to seek
him out.

5. He lived in a tawny sandstone palace two kilometres from the
centre of town, at the place where the igneous mesa began to split. A
summer river fed a forest and residual privilege permitted the lux-
ury of a gardener and family, the appropriation of water, and the
maintenance of a very small game sanctuary.

In the British days, the various Nizams and Maharajas had been
afforded full military salutes. The British, with their customary

punctiliousness over protocol and hierarchy, assigned each native potentate a scrupulously measured number of guns. Thus, powerful rajahs like those of Jaipur and Baroda enjoyed full twenty-one-gun salutes, and the no less regal but less prepossessing rajahs of Cooch Behar and Gwalior and Dewas Senior and even Dewas Junior (whose one-time employee, a reticent young English novelist, introduced Gibbon to the royal reading room) were granted fifteen, or twelve, or eight guns. The Rajah of Udirpur, grandfather of the current resident of the Tawny Palace, had been assigned a mere two guns on the imperial scale. He was therefore called the Pipsqueak Rajah, or Sir Squealer Singh, for the twin effect of his popgun salute and for the only worthy attraction in his district, the notorious Temple of Rats. It is not written how Sir Squealer, a genial and worldly man by all accounts, felt about his name or his general reception.

The grandson, Freddie Singh, occupied two rooms in the sealed-off palace. In those rooms he maintained the relics he'd inherited: swords, carpets, carvings, muskets, tiger-claws, daggers, and the fine silk cords designed for the silent, efficient dispatch of one's enemies. Freddie Singh's private armoury was as complete as any rajah's but no visitor ever saw it. He kept in touch with his subjects, or those few hundred who still acknowledged his rule, and kept out of the way of the State, District and Conservation authorities who actually ran the town.

He had been out of the country once as a young man, then just graduated in business administration from the Faculty of Management in Ahmedabad. The First National City Bank (India, Pvt. Ltd.) had hired him as a stock analyst, and after two years of the fast life in Bombay, he'd been sent to an office in Rome, then Paris and finally New York, to learn stocks and bonds and how to trade in futures.

Those had been the beautiful years of Freddie Singh, those years on the Strand, in the Bourse, on Wall Street, an exiled princeling, smelling of licorice.

6. She and the baby – a rugged little chap, half-Pathan by the look

of him – opened up a room on the second floor, assisted by the old Royal Groom and Keeper of Polo Ponies (now reduced to cook and gardener and feeder of the royal animals), his widowed daughter and her very small daughter who became a companion for young Pierre-Rama.

She seemed to bring some order, perhaps some beauty, into Freddie Singh's life. He no longer sat in his armoury, sipping tea by candlelight. For the majority of people in his ancestral city, the Rajah (though still a youngish man) was either a relic or an embarrassment. When he at last took the unwed foreign mother as a wife, they were prepared to call her Rani if it pleased him. Other names as well, in front of her but never him. The camel, bountiful in all things, provides an anthology of choice insults. The Rani was made to feel as worthy as the slime off a dead camel's tooth. Weeks, then finally years went by, without her ever leaving the compound.

7. Pierre-Rama was nearly ten when the man and his son appeared in town that cool day in late December. Since the Tourist Centre was filled with bird-watchers, someone asked if the visitor would object to accommodation in the Rajah's palace? No, he would not. Would the visitor mind sharing the second floor with the beautiful White Goddess? No, decidedly, he would not. Would he be patient with the Rajah, who, if he could not marry his guests, would often confer upon them land deeds or Moghul miniatures or dusty carpets that had been his grandfather's privilege to bestow, but which now belonged to the State? Yes, he would be patient with the old gentleman.

They put the man and his son (a frail lad given to sneezing in the dust and to whining for the newly outlawed American soft drinks) in Youssef's camel-drawn cart and drove them to the gully-hugging yellow palace. They made their own way through the garden to the main gate, and pulled on a rusty chain to alert the *chowkidar*.

It was the Rajah, clad in pyjamas and a shawl and smoking an English cigarette, who opened the door. He was younger than the guest, a vigorous man no more than thirty-five, with a head and mane of glossy curls, a rounded face and rubbed, rounded body that glowed with a kind of polish the visitor had never seen. 'My wife is upstairs. She is just coming down.' He called up from the stairwell, 'Visitors, Solange! Come quickly!' Seeing confusion in his guest when the young woman appeared at the head of the stairs bowing shyly and murmuring 'Bonjour', the Rajah winked and said, 'My wife, the Rani. She is from Cue-beck, in Canada. And from where, sir, do you hail?'

'Winnipeg,' said William Logan. 'In Canada.'

8. That is how, this night in February two months later, under a sky pierced with stars, with meteorites flaring and bright silent things making their way across the heavens (not planes, satellites possibly, if indeed so many had been launched), under a sky that would embarrass a planetarium, a sky that thrills the way the ocean or a mountain range can thrill, a sky that suggests mythologies more potent than any yet devised, the two are talking, have been talking, for hours. She nurses the baby, Jacques-Ravinder, the Rajah's son, four months old, honey-coloured, plump and good-natured.

How perfect a garment is the sari for nursing babies, thinks the man, William Logan. They sleep under a lavender or green or yellow gauze, free of flies and the glare of the sun, the mother sits with her baby anywhere, nurses him in a crowd with only the little toes peeking from the crook of her elbow to give the act away.

Such is the posture that night. Logan talks. The Rani listens. The Rajah is almost asleep in his wicker chair, contributing nothing but his benign royal presence. The older boys run through the palace undisturbed, chasing rats, confining them when possible to the unused rooms.

9. The stars over the winter desert are mythologically potent tonight. The sky is an ocean, thinks William Logan; I could watch it forever. The Milky Way is a luminous smear, meteorites rip and tear, blue-white stars glitter like messages. There is no sound in the universe but the sucking of milk.

Logan is speaking. 'Now this is a night for sea-turtles,' he says very slowly, because English is the Rani's last language, the one she learned here, with a local accent, from the gardener and his widowed daughter. Sea-turtles she does not understand, but lets Logan go on. Freddie is always there to translate.

'When sea-turtles are hatched, they have maybe twenty minutes to memorize the exact location of their birth. Their exact twenty feet of sand, in the world. And these are among the stupidest animals on earth – can you imagine?'

'That is amazing,' she says.

'But I've seen them down on the beach at Grand Cayman. Caribbean sea-turtles. The old she-turtle waddles ashore and digs a deep trough about fifty feet up from the water. And she drops in her eggs and pats down the sand and goes back to sea.'

'That is beautiful,' says the Rani.

'But they don't make it, see. No, no, the natives hide behind the trees, waiting for the old turtle to lay her eggs. They are too tired now to move....'

'Yes, I am knowing that tiredness....'

'And so the natives attack them, turn them all over on their backs. And after a few hours they build fires on the beach and heat iron spikes red hot and then push them under the shell –'

'Oh, Mr Logan, please. This is terrible. No more, please.'

'Do not be upset, Solange,' says the Rajah, snapping awake. 'I too have seen this.' Because they are stupid, nature protected them with built-in star-charts. Their specialization is a form of stupidity, just as a stupid man will keep repeating his mistakes.

A long silence ensues. 'I have seen skies like this only up north,' says the Rani. 'The nights on the Black Sea and on the Caspian and in the desert of Kandahar and in the mountains of Kashmir were all like this. I could not live without stars like this. It is a head full of jewels, the people say. And in the monsoons when the stars are covered, the people say the camel has closed her eyes and people get sick.'

Mr Logan had not yet spent a monsoon. He wondered how Freddie knew about sea-turtles, coming from a desert in India. He remembered the hundreds of hatchlings racing across the beach like fiddler crabs, the hundreds of birds, the natives with baskets.

The elemental odds against survival had never seemed clearer then.

'Ten minutes to implant those stars, then a mad dash across the sand, and then he hits the ocean with all its monsters. All it knows is how to get back to this lone beach to spawn. The brain clamps shut and it lives on instinct for the next 300 years.'

'That is very beautiful,' she agrees.

'We are the only animals who can get so lost, Mr Logan,' says Freddie Singh.

Under the sari, the baby is shifted to the other breast. For several minutes they watch the meteorites and the steadily moving things that the Rani thinks of as extraterrestrial.

'When our geese are flying south,' says Logan, 'it is said they can hear the Gulf waves crashing on the shores of Texas and they can hear the Atlantic surf in Ireland. From Winnipeg, or Montréal.'

The Rani says nothing but she feels that she has travelled as unerringly as any turtle or any goose and that even tonight she could hear every voice in every language that had ever been spoken to her. This man Logan, a countryman, is over-impressed with the brains of lower animals.

'You are a restless man, Mr Logan,' says the Rani.

10. The three-block frontage of William Logan's birth was Stiles to Raglan, between Portage and Wolseley, in the city of Winnipeg. Though life had stretched him, he often returned to that original scene, in his memory, to the house built by his father on land on the Assiniboine, purchased by his grandfather. In his way he had swum the world ever since. He had lost his bearings.

He had been in Montréal in 1967, living in Westmount and working in textiles. He'd just been divorced. He was thirty that year with a two-year-old boy and he remembered Westmount Park, the library, the sandboxes and the slides. He was, then and now, a tall, lean, bald, elegant man – in textiles, after all – walking slowly, fingers clutched by his little boy, eyes alert to the idle young mothers, so rich, so confident and attractive. They shared an idleness those afternoons – he was frequently in and out of Montréal and found himself with half-days to kill – there was a power in being the only man in the park, with a sturdy little child.

In the ten years with his mother after the divorce, the child had grown less sturdy. He was better now. Logan remembers a day when a new adventure began, when he was sitting at a reasonable distance (but on the same bench) from a blond, maturing woman in a lavender sweater. It was late April, perhaps snow still was pushed in ridges but the earth was dry and dusty. A little girl, pursued by an *au pair* girl, ran to the lady and took a good long look at William Logan.

'Mama, that man is *bald*,' said the little girl.

'Damn,' said the mother.

Logan, who'd never minded his baldness or the reputation it carried, found it a handy prop in establishing his essential harmlessness with younger women, said, 'That's okay, out of the mouths of babes, etc.'

The mother straightened the little girl's jacket and motioned for the *au pair* to take her back to the swings. 'Oh, it's not that. It's that now I have to sleep with you to restore your almighty male ego.'

'Pardon me?' He'd been out of the country.

She gave her address – a brick house on Lansdowne, just up from the park.

The Rajah stood and poured a final cup of tea.

The baby was sleeping and he took him back to the palace and bade his guest good night.

11. 'I'll never get back,' he says.

'To Montréal?'

'To Winnipeg. Not that I want to. I can't anyway. I'm a fugitive.'

The Rani is not disturbed. He has established his essential harmlessness.

'Tell me about the lady on Lansdowne,' she says.

He sips slowly. God forgive me, thinks William Logan: she reads minds and her breast excited me though she's my hostess, a Maharani, and nursing an infant.

The lady on Lansdowne was Hungarian. Thirty-five and very beautiful and bold and angry. She was an actress and her husband had left his wife for her. He had much older children and that obnoxious little girl.

'Her name was Laura,' says the Rani. 'Now, Mr Logan, tell me about the *au pair* girl.'

Before he can answer, he remembers it all. My God, he thinks. He'd lived long enough, accumulated enough points of reference, for his experiences to start collapsing, growing dense with coincidence.

'You looked familiar the first time I saw you. Solange – of course.'

'That day in the park. You called me the *au pair* girl but I noticed you alone in the park and I watched Mrs K watching you and she asked me, did I think you had a wife, and I could see you were both very experienced in the world ... I was not, not at all. I wondered how you two would get together.' She took a long breath, and wrapped the sari-end over her head.

'You speak a lot more when your husband is gone.'

'My husband is never gone.'

She listened awhile to jackals on the plain, the leathery sway of palms in the desert, the distant clatter of wooden wheels, a cart and camel over cobblestones.

'May I call you Solange?'

She pondered the question longer than he thought necessary. 'I cannot stop you.'

'Then what are the chances of our getting together? Surely it means something, no? It can't just be' (he thought of the stars) 'coincidence.'

'Perhaps you are too restless, Mr Logan.'

'It's just that I don't wait for things any more.'

On his last flight from Egypt to Montréal, Logan had sat next to a pleasant, moon-faced young man bound for Athens, and maybe Montréal. He'd asked Logan shrewd job-hunting questions and Logan had been flattered by his interest. Then he'd asked him what time it was. They were south of Athens. Logan told him and the man jerked into a new posture. He stood and opened one of the Red Cross emergency medical bags that was in the storage area immediately overhead. At the same time, six other young men stood and opened other emergency boxes. *Oh, no,* Logan had thought: the boxes were full of grenades.

There is nothing in the modern world quite like eight days of siege to focus a man's attention on final matters. They had landed a few hundred yards from the hillside home of the Delphic oracle. *Low has fallen the prophet's house,* quoted one passenger. Women and children were released; Logan made his peace. As good a place as any to die; as good a reason as any. His life was a hostage-taking anyway, he was a passenger only, detained by fanatics. He vowed, if he survived, to live his life from that moment on as if the person next to him were a terrorist, as if every package contained grenades, as if every flight would end on a hillside surrounded by troops.

12. Just a few weeks before, but a millennium ago, he had landed in Montréal, flown to Toronto, taken the airport limousine to the door of the expensive school he paid for and asked for Billy Logan, a boy who was a stranger to him and whom he'd come to dislike just a little. He'd taken Billy with him back to the airport and they'd flown to London, bought tropical clothes and Logan had sent telegrams to his boss and ex-wife. *Resign effective immediately ... I have Billy don't look you'll never find us.* He bought tickets to a dozen destinations, under various names. Not merely restless, he'd become impulsive.

Some nights, sleep is an act of will requiring as sharp a focus as thought itself. Under such heavens there can be no sleep. Listening to the Rani is like listening to an Indian woman, only better. It's strange but familiar, and behind it is something he can understand. It's erotic, terribly erotic. He cannot control his love, not for her, not for his host, not for his child; he wants to displace the Rajah; he feels at last he has found his home.

In the second week of residence at the Tawny Palace, Logan had boldly proposed to the attractive lady who did his rooms, the gardener's widowed daughter. Perhaps she had not understood; it was instead, her daughter, an exquisite child of – what, thirteen? – who had appeared. And then to say to the girl, 'No, I meant your mother' when she had presented herself so wondrously to him would have offended his morals in some new way. To turn from beauty is a sin, thought the new William Logan; to refuse the daughter would embarrass us all, and be insulting, he feared.

But he had not intended this, any of this, and there could only be one honourable way to act. To enjoy the love of the girl and to try to love the mother. What incredible complications this would lead to, William Logan could not say: only that he was ready to face them. Somehow, marriage was expected, perhaps to the widow. The adjacent space, he had learned, may always be evil, or it may open into the next world, the next level, a higher existence. The girl comes to him after bathing while the mother prepares his lunch. The Rani and Rajah, he feels, have no suspicion. It is a very private, second-floor affair. The daughter must know – though she has never asked – that in the evenings after the main meal has been cooked and the sweeper has cleaned the rooms and she has washed the dishes, that her mother returns, laden with fruits and a small clay pot of sweets, makes tea, then lies beside him.

Is this corruption? At one time he would have known but now he cannot say. He feels at times that he has entered a compact, nothing down, no interest, small monthly payments, but that an unpayable price will be extracted. It is like a nightmare in which he is ice-skating out on the Assiniboine, and he can feel the dark waters oozing from the slashes of his blades; there is still time to skate ashore but a wind is pushing him out to the black open water and he can't turn back.

13. Freddie Singh sits in his armoury, wondering if this is the night. He has come to like the visitor. The boys have become inseparable; there is hope for the boy. But Freddie Singh is still the Rajah of the Tawny Palace; he knows what happens on his grounds as his grandfather once knew what happened in his larger *durbar*. He knows that an uprooted man is the principle of corruption and will spread it wherever he goes. When you announced yourself

from Canada, the Rani said *get rid of him immediately* but I could not. You needed rest, just as the Rani had needed rest. But she has healed, and you have not, my friend.

The people here know of dualities, of coincidence. Every day they see the sand turn to embers. Every night to ice. Ten months of the year, never a drop of water. Two months, walls of mud.

The Rani arrived in India with a friend, another girl from Lévis, in Cue-beck. But the other girl met a handsome Frenchman at the airport and the Rani struggled onward, to the desert. Her friend followed the handsome Frenchman to Bangkok, Hong Kong, Djakarta, Nepal. She loved him, she cooked for him, she became his slave and she helped poison people for him, maybe dozens of young travellers, like her, like the Rani. She will die in jail. She was not evil, not born evil, but she had become lost.

We have known others, thinks Freddie Singh. A fourteen-year-old girl gives birth in a paddy field in Bangladesh nine months after a week of raping, after her mother's rape and murder, her village's rape and butchery. She slashes the wrists and throat of the hated infant, hacks up the body like a fish's, then throws herself successfully on the knife. But someone comes by, picks up the smaller body and takes it to a hospital and the corpse is resurrected. And the baby is adopted by a family in Lévis who name her Marie-Josée and now she's the best student and the best figure-skater in her school.

The people here have seen enough of life to know that coincidence itself is no motive for action. Coincidence on your level, Mr Logan, is a turtle's coincidence, nothing but instinct.

The gardener arrives with a fresh pot of tea. 'You called, sir?' he asks.

'The animals are fed?'

'*Ji*, sahib.'

'Your daughter is sleeping?'

'*Hanh, ji.*'

'You may see Mr Logan now,' says the Rajah.

Coincidence is coincidental, thinks Freddie Singh.

14. 'We have a visitor.'

Logan, sipping the last of his cold tea, turns in his wicker chair.

'Nothing more, Ram, I –'

In the gardener's hands is stretched taut a valuable artefact from one of the desert tribes. In the old days they had joined caravans across the desert, offering their services as entertainers and animal-handlers. And those caravans never reached their destinations. The people were called *thuggis* and they worshipped the principle of creation no less than other tribes, though their ultimate loyalty was to the brother who had died.

Death moves swiftly across the heavens, obliterating the stars at a point just short of meaning, and across Logan's brain like some long-sought solution made suddenly apparent, only to retreat again. He looks up, about to speak, and across to the Rani who now is standing, and turning away. Then he looks down at himself, sees his head perched crazily on his chest and the widening dribble of tea on his luminous white *kurta*, and the stain spreads to fill his universe.

Partial Renovations

JULIA ARRIVED to baby-sit at precisely eight o'clock. The lady was waiting on the front porch, a small concrete slab with a wrought-iron grille. Her name was Shirley Rogers and she was a plain, nervous lady who had just frizzed her hair and bleached it a very bright yellow. The baby, who'd been put to sleep, was called Christopher. The nursery was in the rear on the second floor.

Julia was fifteen and considered a fine baby-sitter, mainly because she was thought of as too stupid to pry. It was a street in downtown Toronto of restless unmarried mothers. Most of them were in their thirties and trying to look younger, like Shirley Rogers. Around thirty-five was when they stopped trying to get remarried and started taking strange kinds of evening courses, coming back around midnight with scraped knuckles, and smelling of things they'd cooked, smoked, or rolled in. The world was divided between women who'd kicked out their husbands and women (like Julia's mom) whose husbands had walked out. Julia often dreaded what the next fifteen years would bring her. She was looking for short cuts. She'd save herself a lot of time and worry if she went through it all in the next four or five years. Twenty seemed comfortably far away. By then she'd be through it all and have a Visa card. At twenty she'd still be fairly young, but at least she wouldn't be stupid and no one could push her around. The only thing she would never do was have a baby. When you had a baby you automatically lost about ten years of living from your life.

Shirley Rogers took her into the kitchen and showed her a counter laid out with apples and oranges and a plate of granola bars. This was the usual thing. Even at Hallowe'en kids on this street got packets of unsalted nuts and granola bars. Then she showed her a pantry loaded with Fritos corn chips, pretzels and licorice whips. 'I didn't know which kind of girl you were,' she said, to which Julia assumed the proper humility. She thought well of her skin and figure but when the time came, she'd rather have corn chips than an apple. There were Cokes in the fridge and Mrs Rogers said she didn't mind if Julia took a beer if that was usual with her. Christopher was a sound sleeper and on no condition should he be disturbed.

The house smelled slightly of talcum powder and baby oil. Mrs Rogers' assertiveness class lasted till 10:30, then she'd go out for coffee. She'd be back by midnight. She had a taped answering machine attached to the downstairs telephone. Julia was not to answer the phone unless it rang three times. That would mean it was Mrs Rogers herself ringing through. Julia told her not to worry about coming back. It was a summer weekend and she could sleep in.

None of the women on the street who had hired Julia would have called her curious or even intelligent. In fact, she was famously stupid on the street, since it was a very well-educated block. But curiosity was her only pronounced passion. She was curious about the physical arrangements of men and women. Not the sexual thing, which was something she knew about, but how they accommodated each other for months and even years in some cases. Over on Marlborough Place she'd read a scroll hanging in a bathroom. It said that marriages were either benign or malignant. You could live with them till they got uncomfortable or unsightly, or else you had to cut them out immediately and hope you got it all. Most of the women she baby-sat for had interesting ways of dealing with men. No matter how hard they hid the evidence, Julia usually found it. Some of them had so many men they had to post timetables in their closets. Her own father had wandered off a long time ago and her sister had just separated after seventeen months of marriage, so Julia knew she'd probably get married to the first guy who turned her on and really wanted to, and then they'd fight and they'd get a divorce.

Her mother said that what killed marriage was having to live together. The more you saw of a person, the more you were sure to hate him. This was also the case between Julia and her mother. That had been the case between her sister Stephanie and Rodney. Stephanie said that if you were the kind who had to have a man around, you should at least housebreak him to show up only when you called him and to leave when you told him to go. Even Stephanie said she was off men for a while, which meant she was cutting back not counting Rodney, who was still around.

Julia liked to open drawers and feel men's clothes. She found them surprisingly soft for the kind of work they had to do. It bothered her that she liked the sound of men in a house. There hadn't been any in her mother's life since her father had left. She trusted their sounds in the bathroom. Her father had always let her stir up the lather in his shaving mug. She liked the dull plunk of the wooden brush handle on the thick glass mug. She would probably marry the first guy who still shaved that way. The earliest memory she had of her father was of him standing over the toilet bowl every morning. She would make the biggest circle with her arms that she could and her father would pee right through it.

Mrs Rogers got a lot of phone calls, which the tape took down and held. She didn't seem the type for so many calls. She must have been at least thirty-eight, and the way she curled her hair and bleached it and dressed in CHUM t-shirts made her look even older. She was flat as a board on top, but getting soft and squishy down below. The thought of Mrs Rogers without any clothes on and doing it with Mr Rogers or whoever was disturbing to Julia. Almost anything that had to do with bodies and babies struck Julia as gross. Bodies made her think of the word 'disrobe' which had to be the ugliest word she'd ever heard. The first time a doctor had asked her to disrobe for him she'd known that she was old enough to start causing trouble.

She knew about taped answering machines. Her father had one, and whenever she visited him he made a special point of turning it off. He told her it was for business messages (he was a salesman), but Julia managed once to hear a full day's tape and it was very different. One lady called five times from places all over the city saying, 'I'm on Queen Street, you bastard, and I saw you take that Chinese chick out to lunch.' On the last tape she had threatened suicide if her father didn't call, and since her father was taking her to a movie that evening, Julia had erased the whole tape. She often wondered what the woman had done. She hadn't sounded right for her father.

Shirley's messages from men were very short. 'Hi, just me. Catch you later.' Then the same voice a few messages later, with noises in the background like boxers in a gym. 'I'm waiting, Shirl. You've got half an hour, then I split.' Julia loved listening to voices like that, to harmless anger she could cut off and replay till it sounded funny. She imagined the guy in a cage behind thick glass, snarling and pounding the glass, while a gang of school kids and their Chinese teacher sat in front of him, eating their box lunches and throwing popcorn like at the zoo.

Another voice, a lady this time, had called a dozen times. First sort of chirpy with a recipe she'd seen. Then with an idea she'd had about a vacation trip, just the two of them, no men. Then in tears, 'I'm not doing well with my life, Shirl,' she said. 'Sometimes it doesn't seem worth it any more. How come you never call me, Shirl? What did I do to you?' Julia didn't like complainers and so she erased it.

By 10:15 she'd had her fun downstairs. The baby was probably wet, or would be soon. She took a bottle out of the fridge and let it stand in hot water, then went upstairs.

Since they were on the same street, Julia's and Shirl's houses were basically the same. She knew how all the rooms were arranged, where the bathroom would be and where the nursery would be in the back. Of course, Shirl had knocked out walls and hung up bright graphics from Marci Lipman's, but that didn't change the space, which still had only fourteen feet of width. This was a street of old row houses that had once been slums, but which architects had discovered and scraped clean and sandblasted and totally reconstructed. Not Julia's house, of course, which was falling apart. Her house leaked from the roof and around the windows and the kitchen floors were always wet and now were slimy and rotting. Shirl had rearranged her staircase to go up the side instead of the middle, and she'd pushed the kitchen back to the end of the ground floor and made it so small that two people could only hug each other if they got caught in there accidentally.

Julia had to pull herself up the metal staircase. It was narrow and steep and had no landing. And when she got to the top she had to lift a trap door, like a hatch on a submarine, a carpeted manhole cover. She was in a bedroom in a sea of grey carpet and mirrored walls, but she felt she'd been climbing a long way, up the sides of a slick, straight hole. There was a king-sized bed with a grey satin cover and a dresser with a mirror that picked up Julia's image and threw it back a hundred times on the walls. She felt like Alice in that old Grace Slick song.

Around the mirror frame, starting at the lower left, Shirl had wedged a panel of dog photos, taken in colour on a Polaroid. In the background were a group of men and women in bathing suits, sitting around a swimming pool. The dogs were a big Dalmatian and a golden cocker spaniel. At the top of the mirror were gross-out scenes of the Dalmatian mounting the smaller dog and getting stuck. The Dalmatian first was high on his hind legs and Julia could almost hear his whining, and the cocker looked ready to snap. But by the lower right their passion had cooled to the point of not looking at each other. They just stood joined like sausages embarrassed and staring in opposite directions. In the final shot a very muscular man and one of the girls had taken off their swimming suits and were squatting on all fours in the grass with their naked bums touching, just like the dogs.

She wondered why anyone would need to keep pictures like that out in the open. Usually Julia had to pry and pry and turn things carefully upside down before she found the magazines and the letters and the pictures – worse ones than these – that were always there.

She'd delivered papers to most of these houses two or three years before. Different people, of course. She was the only native kid on the block. The street was hers by stealth and experience, though she possessed none of it. She was like an Indian, her reservation fourteen feet of rundown frontage. She was there when the moving vans came and she'd be there when For Sale signs went up a few months later. She'd be there till her mother kicked her out. Her house was unpainted and unrenovated. They didn't have a deck on the back but they did have a real front porch with a roof and a swing, one of the last ones on the street, and her mother even sat on it.

As in a dream, Julia headed to Shirl's bed, to a large ceramic boar's head kept on the leather-padded ledge above the headboard, and she knew even before she lifted it that half of the head would come off and that she'd find a small Baggie of grass sealed up tight, grass enough for a good two weeks of before-and-after smoking up. Above the bed Shirl had framed what looked like a 'Personals' ad from the *Star*, only it was blown up maybe a hundred times so that you noticed the raggedy paper and the ink-skips first, and you had to stand back to read it all. It didn't make good sense, even then.

WOOD BURNING TORONTO DF
SEEKS KINDLING
PURPOSE COMBUSTION
Apply NYR Box 1439

It was hard to make out any exits except for the bathroom, which led out directly without any door. It was all pink tile and mirror and gold faucets, with a standing shower stall that slanted down steeply enough to form a kind of half-tub. There was a bubble overhead, light enough for trees and ferns to be growing from the shower stall and from hooks in the ceiling and from shelves in the corner. The medicine cabinet was huge, wider than the double sink, and there were lotions and perfumes and gadgets inside that Julia had never seen before. There were buffers for nails and for calluses and there were hot combs and hair dryers and all sorts of fancy appliances that spelled out age and boredom to Julia, the hand-held autoerotic devices that were usually more carefully hidden. It made her curious about what Shirley might think of actually hiding, if all these foams and diaphragms and pink plastic machines were so up-front. All in all, it was one of the best bathrooms on the street and after carefully replacing things and wiping off the mirrors, she took a copy of *City Woman* with her into the toilet stall for a long christening.

She almost screamed when she returned to the bedroom. On the bed, loosely propped against the headboard and looking as if they'd been there all night instead of only five minutes, were two giant-sized stuffed dolls, Raggedy Ann and Andy. They had not been there before she'd used the bathroom. The walls reflected a hundred images of a frightened girl, totally alone. Whoever had put the dolls there had *just* done it while she was reading *City Woman* in the bathroom. The dolls had the faces and freckles of Raggedy Ann and Andy but the bodies were very different, since they'd been sewn together and Ann's clothes were torn off and Andy's pants were halfway down. Julia was almost afraid to come near for fear that Andy would reach up and grab her. They were like the marionettes in horror movies, secretly alive and in control of the human-looking dolls around them.

She was aware of the phone ringing, somewhere, then shutting off. She wanted to get out of that room and she started pushing against the mirrored panels. One whole wall was a wardrobe that opened into an enormous closet. Normally Julia loved to search through pockets, finding crumpled dollars in off-season overcoats. She made her way around the huge central island of the bed with its grinning redheaded couple staring up at her, using her fingernails to tap on the glass walls so that she didn't leave a smudge, avoiding the little carpeted bulkhead that was the hidden stairway back down to the living room. The only wall she hadn't explored had to lead to the hallway and the nursery, and probably a couple more guest rooms, so she kept tapping and testing the mirrors with her elbow until one finally yielded.

It was black and musty back there, out of the range of central air conditioning. When her eyes got used to it, she made out rolls of carpet in the hall and stacks of bundled newspapers and somewhere at the far end a final door painted white with animal cutouts on it. She found a light switch. The hallway was much like her own house's, with two bedrooms and a bathroom branching off, and a steep narrow staircase at the far end leading up to the third floor. She started walking.

In her house she had a third floor room, the kind with a bed pushed next to the small attic window. There was only a narrow area under the peak of the sloping roof where she could stand up straight. When people remodelled their houses, that was something they corrected right away. They usually knocked out the back wall and made it a wall of sliding glass, leading out to a sun deck. And they would knock out the little attic window and the wood around it and replace it with one huge solid triangular panel, and they would stick a couple of potted trees behind it. That was one sure sign of remodelling you could see from the street. A lot of people on the street lived more on their third floors or second floors than on the first. In the summer they lived on their decks and in the winter they lived under the third floor slope behind their potted trees and they could look out of their triangular windows and see the CN Tower and some of the yellow neon at Yonge and Bloor. Of course, Julia's little window was on the wrong side of the street for that. She could only look north to the triangular windows across the street. And she didn't have a deck to look out of on the back. Most of the houses that she baby-sat had skylights of frosted plastic that were very good for all their plants. Julia had old floor lamps with frayed cords in her room and she'd wedged her cot next to the little window for breeze and for looking into other people's houses. She'd done that all her life. Looking into other houses was like a hobby with her.

The hall creaked as she walked it. From what she could tell, the two bedrooms (or what were bedrooms in her house) were empty. She opened one of the doors and knew suddenly from the smells she was wrong. She knew the smell of old people's sleeping and smoking and drinking, how they could live in any kind of filth and how they contributed to it. Sour clothes, old smoke, cat smell. There weren't any shades on the windows and street lights from outside and the hall light from inside weren't really strong enough to tell her much. Only that there was a brass bed with a grey lump on it, but no sheets. The shape of the lump told her it was a man sleeping with his arm slung over his eyes the way a drunk sleeps day or night in a coin-wash or in a park. And when she took a step inside, a sharp wooden creak from the window alerted her to another presence in a chair, and to the tiny red nub of a cigarette moving from the arm of the chair and disappearing behind its high upholstered back. An old woman coughed.

The second bedroom was much darker, and it smelled of sickness. A man in an undershirt and striped pyjama bottoms sat at an old plastic dining table. He had long, dark hair but a sunken face and body. Julia knew the look of a heavy drinker. She used to think (applying it to an uncle of hers) that drinking kept old men's hair from falling out or turning grey. That was before she learned that her uncle was only twenty-eight, and had a right to his full, dark head of hair. He only looked like sixty everywhere else. This man, now standing and holding the front of his pyjamas like a wad in his fist, could have been one of her uncles. 'Hi,' she whispered, then closed the door on him. The old bathroom's door was open but the smells from it reminded her of her father's unflushed toilet at the cottage, odours backing up from all the pipes. She passed the steep carpeted stairwell leading to the third floor, and opened the nursery door.

The night light was strong enough. There was a crib, a wicker bassinet, another white dresser with stuffed dolls propped on top. She could see the baby's leg peeking out from under the quilt, but, thank God, there were none of the smells she was so good at detecting. The kid really was a dream. She reached through the crib slats to tuck the baby back under the quilt, then she stopped, just before touching his heel.

Someone was behind her, watching. She expected a strong hand to come clamping down on her mouth and for her head to be jerked back so suddenly she'd lose full consciousness, the way Rodney, Stephanie's husband, had done it to her the first time. She waited, knowing that in this house any kind of fighting back would be useless and dangerous, and she knew she wouldn't be the fool she'd been those other times. She turned instead, slowly, holding the crib with one hand, just to brace herself in case he slammed into her real hard. At least she wouldn't have to put up with a wrenched back. Last time the guy had wrenched her back so hard it was almost *that* that had made her go to a doctor. But she hadn't.

It was Shirl. Julia was prepared for a man, some carpet-person rolled up on the floor in an unlit room, someone who just lay in there week after week in case some girl came walking down the hall. Someone who was awake only at night. At first, Shirl's features didn't seem familiar.

'God, you scared me!'

'I called through. I told you I'd call through when the class was over. You didn't pick up the phone, so I raced home.'

'I couldn't find it,' said Julia. She tried to laugh, it sounded absurd, but she knew that Shirley knew she'd been prowling upstairs. The phones were hidden only up there.

'I told you never mind about Christopher. You're looking after the house. The baby is fine.'

There was a man in the hall, very tall, with hair curled like Shirl's, in a white silk shirt with the top three buttons open. He laid a wide hand with many chunky rings on Shirl's shoulder.

'Let me take care of it,' he said. He peeled dollars from a metal clip, the rasping sound of new bills on new bills – he was the kind who handled only crisp bills, who wouldn't take old bills even in change from Becker's or from kids with a paper route. Money made special noise in hands like his.

Her hands slithered down the crib slats, resting briefly on the waterproof mattress. She wanted suddenly to feel something smooth and reassuring, like baby's skin. She patted the heel.

'Five crisp ones do it?' he asked, forking them over.

This time Julia didn't flinch. Not when the baby's heel wasn't cool to her touch, nor warm, nor anything. It wasn't living. It was cloth. She moved her fingers quickly. No one saw.

'He didn't cry, did he?'

'No,' said Julia. 'You've got a great baby.'

'Boys are so easy,' said Shirley to the man, who seemed to agree. 'Didn't even have to change him, I'll bet.'

'I'd *just* come in,' said Julia. 'I didn't even get a chance to straighten his blanket.'

She took the five green ones and let Shirl quickly close the nursery door and guide them down the hall. The other doors were all closed. 'I *must* do something up here,' she was saying to the man, 'I wanted to spare you an upsetting sight.' He said something Julia didn't catch, but from the jerk of the head she knew it was about her. 'Don't be silly,' Shirl giggled, 'she's only fifteen.' Julia had gone past the rear stairwell and the first closed bedroom door when Shirl called out, 'Where do you think you're going?' Julia turned; she was headed for the front bedroom and carpeted bulkhead.

Shirl opened a door that Julia hadn't noticed, or else had assumed was a closet. 'Just how do you think you got up here?' she asked. She snapped on a light. It was the servants' staircase leading down through the broom closet and the pantry and back down to the kitchen.

'I don't think I'll be needing you again,' she said from the top of the stairs. Julia could hear the hallway creaking as the two of them headed to the master bedroom. Shirl called down one final instruction to make sure the front door was locked on her way out.

She didn't consider crossing the street and going home. She had some money and the night was hot and she hadn't eaten and Yonge Street was just a block away. There were nights like this one when all the things she thought she knew seemed worthless and she felt unwelcome even in places that she thought were hers. She felt so light and empty that she could blow away and no one would know that she'd ever been born.

It was only midnight and boys were calling for her from their cars. After a doughnut and a Coke, she took a ride with some boys who said there was a party they'd heard about somewhere on the Danforth.

Sweetness and Light

I HAVE LOOKED into the face of love, and it is black. Black as well are its hands and limbs, and the rest is uniform grey. Up close, there are scars. Tense and silent, tail erect, he paces the railing of my balcony, snapping the buds of the hibiscus that stud the vines stretching to the roof. Baring ferocious incisors, shocking as a bat's, he hisses, then seals his mouth and slowly blinks. I read into his closed, wrinkled eyes a weary tolerance of my presence. He cuffs a female half his size, upon whose back rides an indifferent child – what are his women called, cows? mares? sows? Those clinging little beasties – are they pups, kits, calves? I am out of my element here. My element is, or was, language.

I call him Boom-Boom, and not just for the avalanche of bodies and branches he unleashes on my tin roof at dawn. His harem tears fruit and vegetables from the garden I've tried to raise. Fierce Boom-Boom, liege and pillager, extracts his ten percent on a daily basis.

The flowers – hibiscus, azalea, roses, bougainvillaea – what are they for my Lord Boom-Boom? Appetizers, sherbet to clear his palate, a lozenge, dessert? None of his harem brings him blossoms; these he nips himself. He makes the buds of flowers seem the most extravagant pleasure in the universe. Pink lips unsheathe to surround the bud, tongue circumnavigates the boll, parting its tightly-folded head which he licks at first like a delicate cone, then chops tight to the stalk where ants then rush to stanch its syrupy flow.

Boom-Boom surveys it all, regally, from my cool stone veranda. I've drawn up behind him, close enough to admire his battle scars, to watch the muscles twitching, to see the salt-and-pepper glint of his middle-aged muzzle. We're coevals, my liege and I. I stare down with him at my trees and rows of garden while his women patiently dig up my carrots, bend and break my beans. We're in this together, the harem-keeper and the bachelor bull. Once he whirled and swiped a sticky hibiscus blossom from my extended hand, breaking the skin.

Accidents will happen.

He's watching his women.

Despite everything, I think of monkeys as essentially playful, dolphins of the trees, not territorial scavengers. I wish I still had children to show them to. A wondrous thing, monkeys on your porch. 'See, Bayard,' I would say, rolling back the clock twenty years, 'he wants to play. He wants to be your friend.'

Two years ago my bride and I made a honeymoon visit to a ruined palace at the desert's edge. On the cracked and pitted parapets of the emperor's walk, an old guide had whispered, 'Now I am imparting erotic informations, saar. Maybe the lady should not be hearing...'

'She can take it,' I said.

We were staring at the maze of old *zenana* walls, Rajah Singh's stockyard for twenty-two brides and 600 concubines.

'Seven feet tall, saar,' the old guide intoned, reaching above us to an imagined canopy. 'Four hundred pounds,' and his arms fluttered buoyantly over the hot stone railing. Then, sliding closer to me, dropping his voice, he giggled, 'Penile member, saar, twenty-four inches.'

My bride tittered.

'Jesus, Meena, two feet! How about that. If he couldn't slam-dunk, maybe he could pole-vault.'

My young bride's bosom strained that day against her sari, one breast pressed tight against the discoloured marble, the other flaring in profile from it. How like a painting she seemed, how eternally erotic, the scene enacted a thousand times in catalogues and collections: '*Maid on Parapet Awaits Her Lover.*' Elephants at a distance, camels against the dunes, and I, the would-be Rajah, clutching his Sure-Shot, staring down at the empty breeding pens and wondering, which will it be tonight? One of my experienced courtesans who knows the hundred ways of drawing ecstasy like clear water from a dry well, or one of the shy and painted virgins borne on camel-back as tribute from the villages, who, in their ardent innocence, their exquisite accommodations, can kindle fire from a dampened old stick?

'Saar, a gratuity?' the guide tugged my sleeve.

They are gone by mid-morning, and I am alone with Baba, my father-in-law, under the fan in my private quarters where a serving woman brings me tea and a banana for breakfast and later, yoghurt and fruits sprinkled with coarse sugar. Twice a day an old gentleman in khaki carrying a jute sack tinkles his bicycle bell and drops mail in the wooden box. I can spot my bride's airmail letters from way up here on the veranda where I read and snooze the days away.

At night, after Boom-Boom and his harem make their evening appearance, I change into a clean devotional kurta and pyjamas and sniff about on all fours, thrusting my head into the thick bougainvillaea vines where snakes have been rumoured to hide, and caress a nodule with my lips and tongue, to suck a bud into openness. I have crunched my share of hibiscus buds, and they are pungent as leeks but fragrant, too, like Indian desserts, indescribably flowery. There are always new buds, freshly opened by morning and these I leave for my Lord.

I am what I am, a gaunt baritone with paranoid tendencies, a widow uncomfortable in his body. Not from my lips will you hear gender-shading: no widower I. In this phase of my life, I insist on absolutes.

2. This phase of my life I owe to an engaging teen-ager by the name of Boom-Boom Karakas. I have seen pictures of his room in happier days, his drums and a trophy-case. He is the son I never had: athletic, outgoing, a bit madcap. I have even met the lad, a direct descendant of Genghis Khan on his father's side, though the mother is a bit of a mutt.

I have shaken the hand that U-turned a Camaro across three lanes of the Eisenhower Expressway, down four miles of the northbound lanes warping an errant tapestry through a woof of horns, then plunging like a spawning salmon up the headwaters of a pinched suburban stream. Caroline, heading to O'Hare to pick me up, flipped him like a grizzly flicking a salmon from a shallow gravel-bar, gutting the Camaro from bumper to tailfin. He popped from the dorsal seam like a lichee from its skin. Our car sustained barely a scratch, just a folded fender and a starburst of shattered glass. It was a bloody spawn.

It went better for the boy that he was legally sober and not on drugs. He'd merely been watching old 'Sweetness' himself, Walter Payton, hitting the holes, accelerating, picking up his blocks. He snapped his fingers, kicked his heels and sang, 'I can do that!' They called it 'the Sweetness defence,' the surge of misplaced glory a high-school fullback must feel, finding the seam at night without lights, cutting back against the grain of onrushing cars and trucks, dashing the wrong way down the Eisenhower. No jury would convict, not after the Super Bowl. He'd done it safely, as the phrase went, many times: down the Eisenhower, up the Stevenson, across the Ryan.

Fiction, I'd always taught my students, is a sealed realm of pure and beautiful justice. A justice-dealing machine. The great novel exposes hypocrisy, tests every pretence; that is its only comfort. There are agents of savage justice in this world, most of them outlaws, many of them evil. I'd spent a lifetime teaching students to respect and even admire existential cowboys like Boom-Boom Karakas, the Belmondo of Brookfield Estates. My training in literature, which I took as training for pertinent realms of life and death, told me there was a string in there somewhere. Find it, and follow it through, no matter where it leads. To a ruined estate in Uttar Pradesh, crouched among the monkeys, seems entirely logical.

At that hour of the night, Caroline would have been far beyond the legal limit. I always figured our next sabbatical would be to a dry or expensive country, an academic's Al-Anon. Not that anyone could guess. She was always presentable. And since she was merging into the Eisenhower that night in the proper lane at the proper speed, and she was grey-haired and dressed in a wool skirt and a Scottish sweater we'd bought at Heathrow a few months earlier, they never took a blood sample. I spent three hours in the United Terminal, then took a taxi home, where the police were waiting.

She looked like the wife of a small-college president. I knew her suits and dresses by name: 'Wear your Oberlin sweater,' I'd say, 'your Denison suit.' Knox, Carlton, Bowling Green – the names roll before me now like cherished phrases of a dead, devotional language. I'd lectured in just about every college in the Midwest, been met in every poky airport, gotten liquored up in their gracious guest houses, and always put on an adequate show. We knew their institutional odours, saw them all as choices once offered but never taken, affairs not entered into, enmities spared.

She seemed dressed for a perpetual country auction, under a crisp autumn glaze. Something about her bottled ruddiness suggested high New England, a bright but blustery day with falling leaves. 'I'll bet you're a Smith girl!' one of my colleagues bubbled on first meeting her, 'I'll bet you knew Sylvia Plath!' She stayed trim, but not svelte, more sporting than sexy. She was credited with fitness, but actually she just never ate. People assumed we lived on a country estate and commuted to campus from Wisconsin, perhaps. They came to me with bizarre requests about breeding their dogs and stabling horses. We actually lived in a late-fifties suburban development north of Evanston. We were reclusive because of Caroline's social unpredictability. She would start crying at dinner, or she would drop the crystal. Or fling it against walls, giggling.

In all fairness to myself, I could have passed for a small-college president. I used to wear corduroy jackets and cashmere turtlenecks. My hair turned silver fairly early, as did Caroline's, so we were always thought of as young-at-heart, good-sport senior citizens. On the night of Boom-Boom's intervention in my life, and termination of Caroline's, we were only forty-eight.

'And I almost made it,' he lamented. 'Your wife panicked, professor, and that's the truth. Now I'm looking at a two-year suspension of my licence – where's the justice in that? It's not going to bring her back.' He'd repressed his remorse so deeply, and continued to behave so normally – which is to say objectionably – that the therapists were worried about his recovery. They suggested reserving some of my settlement money for his treatment, should traumas ever surface.

The lad is clearly a force in the universe, a principle of pure destruction. I've paid my dues, I thought, let others pick up the bill. 'Your Honour,' I said, 'I have talked to this boy. He has not publicly expressed the grief I know he feels in his heart. I know these things; I am a literature teacher, a trained observer of life. The Arrangers of the Universe are behind this boy. I support his petition to retain his licence. It is unlikely he will play the Walter Payton game again.'

Let there be no inhibition in the free exercise of his will, I said. Let the rain forests fall, the seas run black. The Court was impressed by my compassion. An act of Christian charity, according to his lawyer. His mother threw herself on my neck. His father wrenched my hand and shoulder. The boy said, 'You're okay, professor.' I left the courtroom worth slightly over five million dollars.

3. 'Three children,' Caroline used to say, 'one of each.' She knew how to carry off outrageousness, sounding just a pinch British, despite having come from Cincinnati.

Carl's in Ophthalmology at Iowa Hospitals; Renata's a young Boer in the Stanford Law School. It's Bayard, child of my Faulkner period, San Francisco's 'Cecil Beaton of Heavy Metal,' who had been our only problem. Now it's his problem. He enjoys being up there with hang-gliders and race-car drivers, in a very special uninsurable risk-group. 'And you always thought I was a sissy!' he laughs.

By day, he's a landscape photographer, doing gardens of the rich and idle. At night he haunts the bars. He's the most debauched twenty-one-year-old I have ever met. He's said no thanks to his future. He gets messages on his telephone service: catch the overnight to Tokyo. KISS needs a glossy.

My question now is, what did we do to deserve Carl and Renata – stodgy even for these constipated times? Carl's friends – other residents in Ophthalmology – could start a Rotary Club of Health Care Professionals. The world is an eyeball and music's for the waiting room. He's twenty-six and getting bald. His girlfriend has three children.

For this I bought twenty years of season's tickets to the Chicago Symphony? For this I refused a television set till they were out of high school?

Renata is also doing well. She's in her final year of women's law. A partnership is guaranteed. I used to melt when she called me 'daddy.' Now she holds me responsible for Caroline's unfulfilment; hence her drinking; hence her accident. It is not comfortable to be called a murderer by the only person, until my bride, who had filled my whole heart.

Bayard you know about. I wish he could be here now. He revels in the debasement of love's design, he knows the shape of love's deformities.

I was becoming a curmudgeon. I was forty-eight, rich, single, and disaffected. My university offered, in their phrase, 'compassionate leave'. I sold the house and made a quarter-million on the inflationary ride. I put everything in mutual funds and started pulling out the equivalent of an endowed, Ivy-League chair. I moved into a north shore apartment with twelve-foot ceilings. I spotted Saul Bellow at our local pharmacy.

Before Caroline's death, the most exotic thing I had ever done was teach in Teheran for a year. I compiled a book while the Shah collapsed. My Iran book was called *Contingency and Character in the Contemporary American Novel*. It attempted to 'locate' (as I used to say) the modern hero in the multiple contingencies of language, history and culture, instead of paraphrasable psychology. The reviewers said it might have been a useful book, twenty years ago, before deconstruction. It's out of print.

And then the Fulbrights called again. Not out of compassion, but with a favour to ask. They were desperate. An obscure college in India had just become Fulbright-eligible, the result of an agreement negotiated by a lunatic who'd never visited the town or the campus. They'd throw in a second year, wherever I wanted, if I agreed to pick up the pieces. 'We owe you one for Iran,' is how they put it. I could be Dr America and Dr Modern Letters in a provincial backwater ('more a backsand, I'm afraid') that had never taught American Lit or anything later than Thomas Hardy.

4. Shri Viswanath Patel University was willed into existence in 1948, five pastel residences and a lecture hall overlooking a cracked griddle of swirling salts, the sunken floor of a dry lake. 'The Death Valley of India,' the Dean-cum-Chairman proudly explained, except when the monsoons made it Great Salt Lake. I was their first foreigner, except for a wayward Uzbek who'd taught *ghazals* by Omar Khayyam the year before.

For those familiar with India, the state is Bihar, a catchment of human misery draining, eventually, into Calcutta. My Fulbright salary, converted to rupees, not to mention the monthly cheques accumulating back in Chicago, probably exceeded the GNP of the entire district.

Viswanath Patel had been a Gandhian. He'd been a 'Sir' but dropped it during the Independence struggle. His vision dictated a college for tribals and untouchables. Some indeed are tribals: handsome, black-skinned men addicted to much adornment. Over the decades, however, ideals have gradually receded. Students come from the middle classes of neighbouring towns, or landowning families of surrounding villages. Despite reservation clauses guaranteeing their admission, tribals have set up trinket-stalls around the college, selling bows and arrows, drums and carvings made of bone. 'Backward castes' do the cleaning and heavy work. The land they beat a living on, by netting fish or raising sorghum, has been declared arid, saline, and terminally leached.

Yet, still, things grew. I arrived just after the monsoons, when the lakebed was already drying and my students were busy ploughing, planting and adding manure. I was given an 'apartment' in the guest house, a furnished room with a fan (though electricity was rarely available), and a bathroom on the Indian model with a hole in the floor between metal stirrups for squatting or taking a standing aim. There was no running water and no kitchen, but I did have a bell, attached to a grey-haired and elegant-looking gentleman who'd once worked in a Calcutta club. He seemed to be on duty twenty-four hours a day. His name was Dhiren.

He had a daughter named Meena.

I had asked for, and been graciously assigned, a graduate seminar in American literature. Every word in that sentence should have quotation marks around it. Once a week, a man vaguely familiar as myself (less and less so as the winter wore on and I dropped my Western clothes, grew a beard and lost forty pounds on Dhiren's fruits and yoghurt), called 'I', stood in a dark, stuffy intimate amphitheatre, candlelit and bug-infested, in front of twenty-five women ranging in age from fifteen to fifty-two, responding to astonishing questions and remarkable opinions on Time and the Universe, the English language and American Trivia. In my innocence, I had assigned the usual texts, from Benjamin Franklin and the Federalist Papers, through *Moby-Dick* and *The Scarlet Letter.* The books had been shipped, but resold in Patna by the bookseller's agent.

The absence of books confirmed something I had always suspected. For the inspired lecturer, the text is often distracting. That winter by candlelight (electrical supply then being in permanent disruption), I reconstructed American thought, American history, the rise and flowering of American literature. I stuck to the syllabus, and they asked questions and wrote papers on the assigned, but invisible, books.

5. Only the blind could ignore such beauty. It was spring by a Chicago calendar, though the seasons made little impression apart from dry and wet. Forster, being Forster, had noticed the deep-chested, wasp-waisted naked male bodies, the graceful limbs of labouring men bursting with muscle. I, being whatever I had become, noticed the women, faces cast more perfectly, skin more radiant, bodies straighter, yet more womanly, than any I had ever seen.

'How are you finding your students?' the chairman, Professor Narayan, inquired. I was feeling expansive. 'Intriguing,' I said.

'They are not, of course, sophisticated at all,' he apologized.

'I find some of them perfection itself,' I said.

'Oh, sir, you do us too much honour!'

'Some are exquisite.'

This was entering forbidden territory. In the Gandhian world, 'lascivious behaviour' can be revealed in a glance, an off-hand word, an innocent gesture. I was thinking of a girl named Meena who had delivered a paper on *The Scarlet Letter,* or should I say, had delivered a paper about a spirited young woman with a child, abandoned by her timid lover, who confronts him in a forest with her unbroken will and her thunderous determination to preach, to write, and to act. I had mentioned Hester in my lecture; I had even commented on Hawthorne's striking defence of art and independence in a Puritan society.

But in Meena's retelling, the forest was hot and snake-infested, the nefarious minister was a drunken and abusive landlord's son, and the young mother a virtuous girl of the serving-class who had been given to him at thirteen to settle her father's gambling debts.

Unsound pedagogy, you say.

She read her paper by candlelight. I had been sitting beside her at the front desk (a dissecting-table in the college's original design), and I lost myself, first in her tears and outrage, and then quite frantically as I studied the shadows under her sari, imagining her nudity from the midriff folds visible to me, a nudity so tangible that I yearned to reach out and dab the sweat, mash the mosquitoes buzzing her head and drinking from her arms, and to begin the delicious unwrapping of all six yards of that Christmas-coloured cotton.

I had been celibate for nearly two years. I had thought of my Fulbright year in an Indian desert as a kind of sexual Al-Anon, a safe removal from much temptation. I had seen my intellectual life as sterile, my paternity irrelevant, my bloated finances a joke.

This is computer-enhancement fuelled by passion: in the candlelight of a hot March Tuesday afternoon I plotted the intimate topography of a small, dark planet named Meena whose age and last name I had never learned. She had been anonymous and now she had erupted in my consciousness and wouldn't let go.

'Yes,' I said, 'beautifully done. Hawthorne would approve.'

We all had a picture now of *The Scarlet Letter* as a revision of Sita's testing in the forest, of a beautiful woman walking through flames to prove her faithfulness, holding out her hand to a doubting, fair-skinned Ram who had put her through the torture of his suspicions. Hanuman, the co-operative monkey-lord who had guided Ram through snake-dense forests and delivered him safely to the island fastness of Sri Lanka, stepped back into the forest's gloom, his duty discharged.

The oldest tableau in Hindu piety.

But what is this? As Ram approaches, slightly humbled by Sita's purity, slightly abashed by his lascivious assumptions, she withdraws her hand. She clutches the child to her breast. His child, perhaps; Ravanna's child – her abductor's – perhaps. 'Tell me,' Ram demands, but she laughs. He will not beg her forgiveness; he demands that she abandon the suspect child to the monkeys and accompany him back to his throne, where he is fated to rule long and benevolently with her at his side.

She laughs in his face. There can be no justice with me at your side, she mocks. I am not yours to command. I did not resist our enemies for fourteen years in order to follow your orders. I did not walk through flames only to serve you now.

He's enraged. What can he do but rule? What can she do but be his wife? It is their *dharma* and their *karma*, to rule and to serve.

'What can I do?' she cries in rebuttal. 'Preach! Write! Act!'

In Meena's tale, Sita and Mukta, her daughter, stay in the forest. Hanuman retrieves them. Ram wastes away in various disguises, wandering through his kingdom, claiming to be the true king. He is mocked, jailed, becomes a drunk and public nuisance. The throne is occupied by lesser and lesser kings, until it is lost to outsiders.

That was the Meena I had in mind, when I spoke of exquisite women to Professor Narayan. 'There is no Meena in our programme,' he insisted.

'Brilliant and beautiful,' I said.

He was smiling when he corrected himself. 'The only Meena I

know is Dhiren's daughter. But she is a serving-girl! Most unfortunate, what happened. A mishap. Divorced, a bad husband, with a child.'

'Yes, I'm sure that's who I mean!'

He reached out to touch my arm, smiling benevolently. 'No, no, quite impossible, you see. As I have explained, she is not favoured in her appearance. She is very dark –'

'This Meena is very dark.'

'– and a servant's girl.'

'So?'

And that was the moment I fell from respectability. To have found comeliness in a dark-complexioned servant's daughter is to harbour lascivious attitudes, to express attraction where only one kind of attraction is possible.

'I see,' said Professor Narayan. 'This fellow Dhiren is very shifty. He asked permission for his daughter to attend your class. I thought, what is the harm? She may even improve her mind and get her thoughts off her problems. She had lived with her father in Calcutta for many years and developed urban ways. Dhiren became a scoundrel and fell in debt. His wife died, and he fell among bad types. The girl was not unattractive in a village sort of way, and so he sold her to bad fellows. Her husband allowed his friends to use her, for money. Then, in remorse for what he had done, Dhiren came to us and begged for honest work. I felt sorry for the chap, so I created a position. Now you tell me his daughter is brilliant and beautiful. I'm very sorry, sir, very sorry I did not warn you before. You are blameless, sir – I take full responsibility. I must release Dhiren immediately.'

'Fire him and you'll lose your Fulbright money,' I said. Lust and pity guided my words. The girl was Cinderella, Sita, Hester Prynne.

'Sir,' Professor Narayan stepped back now, rocking on his heels. 'Everyone here is knowing her story. If you do not cut yourself loose, the good name of your country will be tarnished.'

I heard myself saying it even before the thought occurred. 'I'm going to marry her, Professor Narayan.'

6. We were of course obliged to leave the college. There were, in fact, two children – a boy seven by the name of Amal and a girl of five ... named Mukta. I have learned that the tent of the universe is pegged by coincidence, and that accumulated coincidence constitutes a pattern. I have learned that after fifty, a man encounters no more surprises, everything is vaguely predictable. By the age of fifty, the millions of random thoughts, the thousands of people we've met, the hundreds of thousands of separate articles, books, words, all begin to coalesce. Our character becomes multiple contingency. Meena also had three brothers and four sisters, most of them in Calcutta living precariously. They, along with their children and widowed in-laws, fifty people in all, began arriving a week after our announced intentions.

Dhiren – now known as 'Baba', my father-in-law, though considerably younger than I, feared that his role of servant might cause me embarrassment. I should note that the college, in its excitement over landing an eminent American scholar (as I was then known) had confused the means with the ends and introduced me as Senator J. William Fulbright. Dignified attempts at reclaiming my identity had only met with hurt and alarm. To avoid further indignities to my high office, Baba proposed a reasonable solution.

He wished to return to his ancestral village in Uttar Pradesh and take up landlording. Many abandoned estates, including the one his own father had cooked for, could be bought for a few million rupees. There would be buildings within its walls for all his children and grandchildren. There would be fields attached and outlying villages of indentured labourers to pay him tribute. I was touched by his seigneurial ambitions. There would be an apartment suitable for the Senator and his bride.

We were married in a Christian service in Ranchi, though neither of us subscribed to that faith. Her last name, I learned at the service, was Kumar, common as Smith. We left for our honeymoon in Rajasthan, to walk the parapets of Rajah Singh's palace, to gaze at the *zenana* walls and lose ourselves in lust, while Baba and the family left for Uttar Pradesh with a line of credit for twenty lakhs – two million rupees.

Perhaps you think me trusting or even simple-minded. I draw your attention to the ballast I've shed in the cauldron of love. If Newton's laws hold true for the moral universe, consider an equal and opposite reaction to the surrender of my name and citizenship, my wealth and whiteness, my tenure and refinement, my three children and a spotless defence of culture and irony wherever they seemed imperilled. Consider the Giddiness of Being that follows when the memory-banks are spilled like water in the sands of Rajasthan.

I was being reborn, you see.

Seven feet tall and proportionally endowed, I waited at sunset on the Rajah's walk for a signal from *the maid on the parapet, awaiting her lover*, my bride. Secrets of the ancients coursed in my loins. My virgin courtesan had never been inside a hotel, had never eaten restaurant food, had never worn jewellery, a silk sari, or even a bra. Had never been taken in a gentle embrace by a man not bent on hurting her.

I have had affairs, yes, with students and with colleagues and with the wives of colleagues, and in all those tangled, expectant moments there inhabits the shadow of an ultimate purpose: what it means to be a man, to escape the old self, and to create something new. Don't look for profundity here, for I am out to extinguish all the markers I took to be normal and within the parameters of the Male American Self.

Those moments were not repeated with my bride.

She met me in the room, in her *Scarlet Letter* sari as I had requested, kohl-eyed, tinkling in her honeymoon gold and jewels. I turned off the air-conditioner. I turned off the fan. She put her hand on the back of my neck, and it was ice cold and trembling. I followed the hand, the thin arm ribbed with bangles, up the smoothness to the elbow, under the sari-end that hid the rest of her arm, and shoulder. My fingers followed the outline of the *choli*, where it scooped in the back and hooked in front and I eased the eyelets apart. Still no bra, no wonder I had not miscalculated a millimetre of that exquisite topography. The sari hid everything from my gaze. My hands slipped down her sides, bare and warm, to where the folds of her sari were nipped by a drawstring. She tugged and it came loose. I lifted the sari and she stood before me in a petticoat and opened top. She tugged again and now my white pyjama bottoms tried to fall unimpeded to the floor but, understandably, snagged.

I sing you no tales of love's disillusionment. Love is not a domestic animal and I have been spared the petty politics of its taming.

We returned to our new estate of marriage on these grounds that Baba bought: a crumbling mansion, servants' quarters, apartment blocks for minor relatives, orchards, animal-pens, and a high wall studded with glass. In one of those servants' pens, Baba had been born. He wept at the memory.

Money-lenders of the last century, fat merchant-princes of Calcutta who dabbled in landowning and the casual chatteling of seasonal labour had built this mansion, deeded these fields, indentured these surrounding villages. A consortium of owners, great-grandchildren of the merchants, now Calcutta wastrels little better than servants themselves except for exalted notions of their lineage, sold their interest to Baba for little more than back-taxes and a transfer fee. Baba hired a tax-official to do his negotiating, which amounted to threats of prison terms and fines bearing compound-interest from the British days, if the deeds were not turned over in compensation.

7. Special effort seemed called for.

In these two years we have reclaimed three rooms of the mansion with paint and wood and plaster, we've unburied an Aphrodite sculpture that rioting Muslims had decapitated in 1947, we've repaired the outer walls and begun pruning the mysterious orchard – snake-choked, hazed with bats and resting monkeys – which should bear sweet lime and mango in a year or two if Boom-Boom's ladies co-operate. In olden times, five villages depended on this estate for inputs and simple justice before extractive greed brought everyone to their knees. Senator Fulbright has used his influence to bring electricity, a classroom, and a dispensary. He's even done some teaching of the servants' children. Gradually, in this life, I am finding my level.

With the possible exception of Baba and Lord Boom-Boom, I am the happiest man I know.

The money for playing both man and god should last another year or two. Meena writes me that her teachers are pleased with her progress, and with Amal's and Mukti's. They are American school children, as she had wished. They live in my north shore apartment with the twelve-foot ceilings. She is the only freshman at Northwestern with an MA (Sir V.N. Patel Univ.) in English literature. She writes that Chicago is very cold this winter.

Perhaps it is all a dream, but if it is, I am dreaming in colour, with a full palate of taste and texture. Boom-Boom and I have learned a game, on his evening visits. We sit on the warm stone balcony, rolling my evening orange back and forth, each of us feigning a bite, holding it close for inspection, pretending to keep it, licking it, then rolling it back. He finds this orange game vastly amusing, and he has permitted some of his ladies and children to join us, each of them rolling fruits or pebbles, licking them, and rolling them back to me.

Then comes the time when innocence ends.

This evening, biting off buds for tomorrow's worship as I always do, tongue parting the crevices between the leaves as Boom-Boom has shown me, lips grasping, teeth in readiness, moray-man in the reef of his bougainvillaea, I encounter the surge of new resistance, of low, astonished lizard-life, the green head no larger than a bud trembling in my mouth, its twitching tail jerking from my lips. My tongue is nipped – it could have been worse – and Lord Boom-Boom swipes once at my face and dashes the poor lizard to the floor.

And then he pushes me aside, for there, lured at last from the ladder of my vines, the giant head appears, awakened from its millennial sleep. My Lord squats on the parapet wall, the snake, its yellowed hood flaring wide, its tongue flicking, launches itself only to fail, to spray the stone with venom at Boom-Boom's dancing feet. The women begin their screaming, their flinging of fruits and pebbles. Hanuman, my guide and protector, dodges and leaps, landing astride the ancient god, pulling it from the forest of leaves and raking its flesh with his claws, battering its head against the parapet. When it is safe, the first of his women, and then I, join the general battle. We leave the snake bloody and twitching, under a pulpy sludge of burst-apart oranges. Boom-Boom studies my face. I read his brown, bag-rimmed eyes, his wrinkled face and cheeks. *This far and no further, O wanderer,* his eyes tell me.

He rises, whistles once, and his troop of women gather. Another whistle and they plunge over the stone railing still moist with venom, and gather again in my garden, to plunder my fields under the watchful eyes of their god.

The Love God

'He greases my griddle,
Chops my meat,
He wets my dreams
He keeps his horses in my stable.'

– 'My Handy Man,' Victoria Spivey

MY EARTHLY FATHER is listed as Lyle Coombs, a beans-and-cotton farmer from Pocahontas County, Arkansas. My mother, Elvina Tulleson Coombs, was a tenant farmer's daughter from outside Tupelo, Mississippi. They had been barren for twelve years of marriage prior to my arrival in 1940. Both were god-fearing Pentecostals and part of my childhood was spent under the eye-smarting swelter of canvas revivalism. I record these facts from my birth certificate in the interest of total candour.

I do not know where I come from. I do not know who I am. In these eerie byways of the self, I know I am the direct descendant of Michelangelo and Shah Jahan. Certainly I fought with Genghis Khan and Alexander the Great. Everyone recognizes me, but no one knows what I look like. Lyle Coombs thought I looked just like him – a scrawny little guy with chest, back and arms so woolly, and a head so bald, you thought he was the victim of some misdirected drug experiment. In the mirror, any given day, I see a fit young blond with a California tan, a swarthy Italianoid with gold chains and wiry hair, an uptown dude, a tweedy professor in Oxford cloth button-downs. I am not certain that I exist, despite the comforts I have taken in others' bodies.

Penny Path, my true, eternal father, was, when I got to know him, somewhat arthritic in the hindquarters from nearly twenty years of hauling and occasional plough-pulling through Lyle Coombs's dense, hill-country clay. Further to my commitment to total candour, I must acknowledge that I am not Penny Path's only child. By his reckoning, which was necessarily dimmed by time and circumstance, he had sired several thousand offspring, though I was the first to assume a general human form and demeanour. He thinks I look exactly like him, but if I did, I'd have four legs and whinny at the mares.

Do not be fooled by outer appearance.

I have the true story of my conception from my mother's telling, though even she is unaware of the full details. She remembers a pinkish cast to a cloudy, late-summer afternoon in 1939. She was on the porch shelling peas into a large wooden bowl. With Lyle away for three days, Penny Path had worked his way nearly to the fence near where the truck was usually parked.

It was a quiet, drowsy afternoon with war just breaking out in Europe, and cotton farmers like Lyle immediately speculating on a rise in cotton prices. He'd gone to the bank in Jonesboro to raise money for his first tractor. Failing that – he was a man accustomed to failure, and the New Deal hadn't transformed much of that west-central corridor of Arkansas into a solid money economy – he was also to see a vet about the care and feeding and cost advantage of breeding mules for labour and either selling or even destroying old Penny Path. To breed a mule, of course, you needed donkey sperm and a scrub mare to receive it. While it was true that Penny Path didn't show much inclination to slow down as the best local stud, and that his bloodlines, though lost on paper stood out handsomely enough in his progeny, it's not as though he was worth all that much, either. He was getting on, and he'd become a mite touchy.

She remembers the heat of that night, alone in bed. The moon burned like an auxiliary sun, worn and scarred and nearly orange till it climbed. Lyle had installed a generator to keep a light on in the shed where he raised a few hogs and chickens, and the house lights were tied to it, along with a radio. She was lying in that moon-bright dark listening to ballroom music from WWL in New Orleans and thinking how much she'd like to have a baby to look after on nights like this, and how much she hated having to go out in the bug-crawly night and unscrew the housefeed from the generator when the moonlight suddenly cut out, as though a giant cloud-bank had moved over it.

Then she saw why. She saw the form of a stranger just standing at the bedroom window. His head and shoulders and half his body filled the window and the moonlight outlined his deep, broad shoulders, sculpted and smoothed the bulges of an enormously strong but totally unscarred body. She said it reminded her of white marble, like pictures she'd seen from Greece and Italy. He looked serene, not frightening to her at all. He'd entered her life the way images enter in a dream, without warning, without even the noise of his breathing.

Now, the house in which I was born was a simple, pre-Depression catalogue item, commonly used to shelter a farm's tenant-family. While it was all on ground level, the bedroom window was still a considerable distance to the ground. The house was set high on a stone foundation, so that Lyle Coombs, for example, a man of normal height, could not be seen from the bed when he walked past the window. She had a good view of the windmill and the fence posts and the roof slope of the outbuildings, but the idea that a human being could even be seen, unless he was standing on a ladder, and that he could fill the entire double-hung windowframe was unthinkable.

He didn't speak. He held out his arms – there were no screens – and my mother went to him. He simply lifted her through the window, holding her out flat in his arms like an offering, and she felt a cool breeze against her cheek and shoulders as a wind came up. She knew she was being borne away at great speed in the arms of a god-like giant, but she could only hear hoofbeats below her, and at a distance. She kept her eyes closed and when he set her down in the highest field under a line of cottonwoods, she surrendered to him with such shuddering totality that she knew her barrenness had ended for all time, like a queen bee after the first and final penetration.

One may wonder how a son learns such facts from his mother, and I can only say I am uniquely blessed in eliciting the most intimate sexual details from everyone I meet. In me they see their fantasies, a man who understands, who has experienced everything and passed beyond all curiosity, all need, all prurient interest. The blankness of my response often leads to deeper engagement and more self-exposure than ever intended.

My mother remembers the aching of her full breasts and my refusal to take them, my preference to hold them in my hand and dangle the nipples over my eyes, to lick and not to suck. I could lie in her lap for hours gurgling to her unbuttoned fullness, tracing each pulsing vein, twanging a few stiffened hairs at the edge of her aureole. She remembers visitors pulling down the ruff of my loosened diaper and seeing an organ there that belonged on a man of heroic proportions, though she, of course, saw only a baby. She remembers the embarrassment of taking me into Jonesboro to the park around the Confederate Memorial, and as she wheeled me in, dogs would begin their humping, tulip trees and magnolias would shower petals on the benches. I remember fishing in the ponds near home, the squirming black balls of catfish larva bobbing around my cork, the copulating dragonflies resting on my line, the canopy of bugs and birds over my head, the clotted flies tumbling from the air.

I remember the night of my conception, and I have it not only from my mother, but from my father himself. My mother knew her experience had not been of this world – she only wondered if she'd been dreaming it. When she dared to open her eyes, she saw only old Penny Path standing under a cottonwood and pulling up clumps of grass. He was an ornery beast and no one had ever tried to ride him. She'd never exactly ridden a horse, having been raised around mules on a Mississippi tenant farm, but she found herself approaching the unsaddled animal in her flimsy night wrap and pulling herself on him, practically lying on her belly over his back and holding tight to his neck as he slowly bore her home. He stopped at the bedroom window without an order being given and she was able to slide off and stagger back to bed.

It is fortunate, in those times and in that Pentecostal home, Lyle Coombs arrived a day early and that my mother, with unaccustomed vigour, was able to lure him to bed and even to engage him in formats that she said she'd dreamed would lead to a pregnancy. Lyle had given up all hope, but still surrendered – he held a nearly Catholic view that the end of sex was procreation, and their sustained barrenness, rather than challenging him to greater effort and frequency, had discouraged him from participating in the whole humiliating activity.

Of course we communicated, my father and I. His true name was Panipat, named for the battleground where Emperor Babar brought the lone true faith to pagan India. His ancestors had boiled from the sands of Arabia, carried emperors east and west, had borne the most regal and powerful men of their times into battle and ceremonies. He had been the private mount of Emperor Shah Jahan; he had watched the building of the Taj Mahal, and his throat had been slashed, along with the throats of eighty camels and two royal elephants to be buried in the tomb at the moment of its completion. He grew to full amorousness as the lead-stallion in Emperor Ranjit Singh's Imperial Cavalry, and bore His Majesty himself, a man of 300 pounds and 200 concubines. He had borne the British to India and Afghanistan and the Crimea, pulled cannon on the continent, and was auctioned off by Scotsmen and sent to Canada and the United States, and sold down river into the beans-and-cotton lands to be used like mules and donkeys.

My father hated mankind. He harboured the hatred of a slave who remembered his kingdom.

In the war years, Lyle Coombs prospered. The old steam tractors of an earlier era rusted near the windmill. 'First came steam, then draft horses, then mules,' said my earthly father, pitchforking a bale of hay at my eternal father, 'now it's diesel tractors, soon's this war's over. This ole son's days are numbered. A stud stallion these days is worth his weight in catfood. Got a pet-food processor been sniffing around. Big ole boy like you'd go for forty dollars, easy.' It was Lyle Coombs's little joke that Penny Path could understand his insults.

Little did Lyle Coombs know the ways of the world.

Like a boa constrictor swallowing a cow, my real father once told me, the days of men are numbered. For the first few months the cow will still be standing, chewing her cud. All she knows (he had a low opinion of cattle) is her tail's too heavy to twitch at flies. A few months later, her hind legs have nowhere to go. A year later, she'll be half digested and still be mooing.

He could not forgive the farmers of Pocahontas County, especially Lyle Coombs. Watching the mares he'd consorted with – just about every available mare in Pocahontas County and some from eastern Oklahoma had been backed into his special stall, for his pleasure. The rough equation of pleasure: a woman weighs a hundred pounds; a mare weighs ten times that. A man's apparatus is what – six inches, he snorted – a stallion's is three times that. Human sexuality held all the appeal of a polyp's budding. Every horse in west-central Arkansas was of his blood – and every mare was now full of mule, mule, his word for all that was foul and degenerate. He'd watched his daughters raped for profit with donkey sperm. Like breeding your wife or daughter to a chimpanzee and calling the monster an improvement on nature because it ate bananas and could swing on trees. He saw his magnificent apparatus for begetting future generations now treated as a joke – 'That thing's 'bout as useful as titties on a nun,' Lyle Coombs would joke, expecting me to laugh along with him.

'Wonder can they geld a stallion? Make a steer out of you and quiet you down some?'

I could feel the heat rising.

'Hey, I'm talking to you, old son.'

Penny Path reared up on his hind legs and in a blast of glory, turned black, white and gold. Tulip trees and magnolia blossomed, branches creaked, cotton bolls burst like popcorn, a roar of animal and insect pleasure deafened the yard. Flies and mosquitoes tumbled around us, too silly from lust even to bite, and the yard turned slimy with a million tiny frogs the size of bumblebees. He'd squeezed life from the soil and from the air.

To quiet Lyle Coombs forever, Penny Path reared up and sprayed us all in the chunky white mist of his immortality. I was drenched, Lyle Coombs swatted his arms in front of his face and raked the horse with his fork. One flick of a foreleg and the pitchfork was splintered and Coombs was left holding a shattered hand.

'Catfood!' he howled, and slithered away over the dying frogs.

I was five years old, in human time.

My father came to me that night. Lyle, with a bandaged hand and fire in his brain, had made sleep in the house impossible. I moved to the barn under cover of dark, scuffing my feet over dead, dry frogs.

Your mother is scrub stock, a rampant hag, said Panipat. I did it to hurt the donkey-man. She has not slept with him in six years without laughing.

'He called the meat-processor,' I said.

I'll be gone by then. It doesn't matter.

'He'll hunt you down.'

The cats are welcome to it, he said. I've hunted tigers, cheetahs and desert lions. All things return to the soil. Whole forests bloom from my turds. Let the great Panipat quietly repose in kitty litter.

'No, you won't,' I said.

I was a determined young man, even at an earthly five. In the revival tents of my childhood, the scariest story of them all, for a young boy, was Abraham's sacrifice of Isaac. My father may have looked more like Esau with his hairy arms, and he didn't have a people to lead or a land to find, but he was an Abraham, secure in his righteousness, founder of a line late in life with a wife who was ageing fast. If his god had told him to sacrifice me, he would have.

Is there a story in which Isaac sacrifices God?

We looked over the available equipment in the barn. There were some steel templates, worn pretty smooth and sharp, but we tested them on Panipat's neck and I couldn't draw blood. We rummaged around for a good blade and found only fragments of old implements that crumbled into rustflakes in my hand. By this time, Panipat was pretty excited about shedding his mortal coils. He planned to walk the earth a few years, on two feet, sacrificing real sex for the exercise of brute human power. Perhaps human beings had compensated for the lack of serious pleasure in their lives. The atomic bomb had just been dropped. The bomb, coupled with the war, had impressed him. He knew a long chapter in human history – the capturing, taming and exploiting of nature, the Age of the Horse – was drawing to a close. It was the chapter that had made him a deity.

We found only a roll of new, strong, baling wire.

He reared again on his hind legs, as he had that afternoon, and as I watched, the hind legs straightened, and the body transformed itself into a man perhaps nine or ten feet tall, with marble skin and glossy black curls, tall as a horse at full extension. It was the body, I know now, of Michelangelo's 'David', this time with his shoulder looped with wire instead of a slingshot. He paid no attention to me, but walked like Moloch himself to the loft-ladder and began to climb. Rungs burst as climbed, the loft planks creaked and cracked as he pulled himself over the edge. Then he stood, and looped the wire over the highest beam, and wrapped the other end tightly around his neck.

He stood, towering above me forty feet.

'Leave!' his human voice rang out.

As he dived to the floor, the body flashed through a hundred incarnations, the changing-room of his immortal soul, then resumed the familiar, equine dimensions. The middle beam cracked, the roof began to sway, and as I stood in the bare clay outside the door, I saw the giant horse, my father, swing twice before me, his legs out stiff, head relaxed at a terrible angle. The wire snapped, then came the thunderous, hundred-year crack of dry timber: down came the beam and loft and tons of hay, and to the screaming of the hogs and screeching of chickens, came the collapse of the barn, lying down and snapping, like cottonwoods in a tornado.

Had it not been for the flood, I might never have fulfilled my destiny. The Army Corps of Engineers, freed between the war and the Korean outbreak, turned its attention to a number of river projects in the South. No river that had ever overflowed its banks was safe, especially not with local Congressmen, with thirty years' seniority, bobbing in the pork barrel.

We had good bottom land, but Lyle Coombs didn't fight it. He let the government buy us out, and took the profit to Little Rock and opened up a cotton brokerage. The house where all this happened and the ditch where Panipat is buried is now a harbour for bass, forty feet under water. We became middle-class and respectable. I graduated from Central High in the first integrated class, where I played absolutely no role of historic importance. That is not my scene. I am the dark shadow of Eros, the part that broke away.

In the way of these things, it was inevitable that I would find my way to Hollywood, the other place where gods mess with mortals and bloodlines get confused. I was going to school in Fayetteville, when some girls from a sorority asked if they could enter my picture in a look-alike contest. 'Who do I look like?' I asked, more puzzled than flattered, because that morning I had looked like a young Richard Nixon in my mirror.

'Oh, come on. You know,' they said. They were giggling. The one with the camera ran her finger down my nose and over my lips. 'Kennedy, of course. I think Bobby more than John, but that's okay.' I took her to bed that night and she called me Instant Replay.

Of course I won. Once my picture was in a Kennedy Look-Alike contest, it was bound to win. It would have won a Khrushchev or Harry Belafonte contest. What the producer had in mind was to cast the president of the United States in a sleazy porno film to be called *The Party of Your Choice*. I starred with the winners of the Jackie Kennedy, Pat Nixon and Mamie Eisenhower contests, doing things, I must confess, that any red-blooded American boy had fantasized about.

The producer was an upstate California lawyer, otherwise respectable. *The Party of Your Choice* was just the beginning. He had plans, once he saw my potential, to bring American classics explicitly to the screen. He loved Hawthorne. He'd studied witchcraft. He saw fresh ways of filming Henry James. He signed me up for *Tom and Becky Get Laid*. He planned a *Sister Carrie* with a quality cast of porno stars that would blow the socks off mid-America.

I should have recognized who he was.

The movies enjoyed a quiet success, even though 1961 was still the fifties. My acting name was Leo Libido. Forces were percolating through the system. They liked my versatility, the man with a thousand faces and a single rampant urge. No one could trace me – my identity was safe. I specialized in aged priests, teachers, judges and dentists – any role where the robes came off. I played hospitalized heroes jerking off (my Gipper's a classic). In *The Home Movies of J. Edgar Hoover* I played Martin Luther King, Jr. and JFK again. Newspapers in Greenwich Village and Berkeley gave me awards. I had a following, in the sexualized underworld.

When my father was dying, I went back to Little Rock. He'd developed diabetes after my mother died, and he was a sorry sight, even enough for my sympathy. It was the week of the Kennedy assassination. He was blind, and reached out for my arm. 'I'm dying,' he said, 'so don't lie to me.'

He clutched my arm and he must have felt its smoothness, for his fingers jumped as though my flesh were coals.

'You know, I always suspected Elvie. She changed so much after you were born. You're not my son, are you?'

I could have brought him a deathbed satisfaction. When he squeezed my arm a second time he must have felt the Coombs-male fur. He was smiling. I sent him to the next world with something to think about.

'I am the son of the horse you knew as Penny Path,' I said.

I think he was speaking to me from the other side. He smiled and patted me once. 'Yes,' he said, 'I suspected as much. So much I missed.'

My rise to legitimacy coincided with Vietnam, the second wave of assassinations, with the acceptance by younger kids who seemed to have been born with attitudes I'd had to struggle for. I was losing my definition in the larger world of American decadence. I couldn't shovel my drugs fast enough into the veins of America. By now I'd given up acting and was writing, directing and producing my own brand of guerrilla cinema. Every Man a Stallion Productions. I produced in film, in photos, in songs and stories the fantasies my women told me. They didn't have to speak, I could read their minds as I passed them in the street.

My old producer came to see me again. He'd changed appearance. Now he was a dapper middle-aged lawyer with long blondish-grey sideburns, dressed in the Beach Boys florals of the late sixties. Dying in Arkansas, he confessed, was the smartest thing he'd ever done. Already he'd forgotten his centuries as a stallion. What he had as a man was quite satisfactory enough – it's not only women who fake their orgasms. It was a new age with new energies, and California men were at the controls.

'Well, dad, I'm not in awe of you any more,' I said.

He was into hot tubs, computers, franchises, singles bars, drugs, disco music and electronics. He'd walked the streets of the Castro District, and liked what he'd seen. Clones of the Love God, he called them. First time in American history a community defined itself by sex. He saw a parallel economy to service a parallel sex.

'What happened to the God who died for love?' I asked. 'Everything I've done I've done in your name. Every Man a Stallion – I've dedicated my life to you.'

'I decided to stick around. Don't be a religious fanatic – what are you, Pentecostal after all? Sex was then. Money is now.'

'I guess I'm very then.'

'Then you're doomed, believe me.'

Who could believe sex was finished? It was the mid-seventies, everyone was leading a swinging life. My movies were almost respectable now, not quite mall-fare, but playing in the cities. Nixon was the president. Available women were losing their lustre. I'd helped sexualize the world, as part of a bargain. I sold my corporations, changed my face and address. Goodbye, Leo Libido. Farewell, Every Man a Stallion. For the sake of children, I decided to get married.

I took the name Elrod Stubbs and married the purest, sweetest woman I could find in Little Rock. She tells me I'm a handsome fellow in his late twenties, which suits me fine. My mirror still plays tricks; I know I'm in my late forties and given my avoidance of exercise, I can't be anything special. Her name is Daisy. We have three children, two boys and a girl. Their chromosomes are stable. They cannot coax bugs and birds and blossoms from the air. We live outside Atlanta. I am a media consultant.

I swear on all that's holy to me – the memory of my true, uncorrupted father who died that we all might lust more abundantly – that I did not intend the suffering I have unleashed. I'd made peace with both my fathers and only wished to be left alone.

That being said I must also confess even sons of the Love God know a mid-life crisis. My commercial life is full of models and provocative poses. Leo Libido remembers it all and can't always banish the urge. We were filming a Coca-Cola ad off the Florida Keys, a parody of *Treasure Island* where the pirate's chest is full of Diet Coke, and Friday is an exquisite blonde in a chartreuse bikini who gets left behind. I found her, alternately, meltingly then stabbingly beautiful. Her name was Felicia.

I was resting in a lawn chair. Felicia came over and crumpled down beside me. I felt the old urge coming on.

'I bet you don't lose out to Coke cans very often,' I said.

She whispered, 'I didn't lose, Leo Libido,' and kissed her fingers and trailed them down my nose and over my lips.

'You're too young to know about him.'

'Try me.'

'How do I look to you?'

'Short, squat and indifferent.'

'My chin?'

'Weak and wattled.'

In her trailer, she kept a sample of every designer drug known to modern chemistry. She changed her moods like hair colour. We fast-forwarded through a Stanislavskian afternoon: as Brando, Belmondo, De Niro, Nicholson. She popped her pills, snorted and shot, to match my changes. We called for instant replays.

On the drive into Key West she said, 'You will, of course, leave your wife.'

I was noncommittal. 'I'm happily married.'

'Say goodbye. I can make problems, you know.'

'What do you want?'

'Love,' she said. Then, quietly, 'Love's gotten too cheap. It needs an edge. I want real love. I want adoration.'

'Ever tried children?'

She snorted. 'Elrod Stubbs, or Leo Libido, or Travis T. Coombs, my boy, I wasn't even a woman till last year.'

I felt my genes collapsing, attacked in the core of my being. I felt a thick, black evil swirling in my veins. 'Father,' I said, 'you bastard.'

'It is the nature of the Love God to be loved. Do not despise me for what I am.'

She led me to a dockside street of dancehalls and restaurants. Jaws dropped, sailors couldn't pucker for a whistle. She was too close to their dreams. We paused outside a darkened, cedar-trimmed bistro called *The Errant Knight.* I could hear the Cole Porter medley inside: 'A New Kind of Love', 'It's All Right with Me.' Sing it, Judy.

I stood outside with Helen of Troy, Nefertiti, Mumtaz; I entered with my father's best and favourite, Michelangelo's David.

'They love me,' he said.

All heads swivelled. His arm was cold and deadly. He turned to me a final time before joining the men on the dance floor. He seemed to be laughing. 'Together, we'll bring back an age of corsets and cold showers. We'll make them pay, won't we, son?'

So, I said later that night to a high school teacher from Cleveland who'd been smiling at me brightly, admiring my profile with its stately Roman nose and lips, come here often?